SHEDROW

To Melissa, with best wishes —

SHEDROW

A NOVEL

DEAN M. DELUKE

Dean M. DeLuke
9/28/10

GREY SWAN PRESS

Publisher of Fine Books   www.greyswanpress.com

Grey Swan Press
www.greyswanpress.com

This book is a work of fiction. Names, characters, places, and incidents are products of the author's imagination and are used ficticiously. Any resemblance to persons, living or dead, is entirely coincidental.

First Grey Swan Press hardcover edition, August 2010

100% acid-free paper

Printed in the United States

Library of Congress Control Number: 2010927308

PERMISSIONS

Tell Me On A Sunday
From SONG & DANCE
Music by Andrew Lloyd Webber
Lyrics by Don Black
© Copyright 1979 Andrew Lloyd Webber licensed to The Really Useful Group Ltd. And Universal/Dick James Music Ltd.
All Rights for Universal/Dick James Music Ltd. In the U.S. and Canada Controlled and Administered by Universal – PolyGram International Publishing, Inc.
International Copyright Secured. All Rights Reserved.
Reprinted by permission of Hal Leonard Corporation

Story of My Life
Words and Music by Jon Bon Jovi and Billy Falcon
© Copyright 2005 Universal – Polygram International Publishing, Inc., Bon Jovi Publishing, Warner – Tamerlane Publishing Corp. and Pretty Blue Songs
All Rights for Bon Jovi Publishing Controlled and Administered by Universal – PolyGram International Publishing, Inc.
All Rights Resered. Used by Permission.
Reprinted by permission of Hal Leonard Corporation

Headline and news article reprinted with the permission of the *Lexington Herald-Ledger,* copyright 2007. Permission does not imply endorsement.

ISBN-13: 978-0-9800377-6-0

10 9 8 7 6 5 4 3 2 1

Acknowledgements

At the first writers workshop that I attended, a three day course given by Michael Palmer and Tess Gerritsen on medical fiction writing, Michael Palmer said of the writing process, "It's hard work." He was right, and my work was made lighter by many mentors and assistants, including the above two masters of the medical thriller. Another master, Robert Dugoni, was invaluable as well. All three authors take part in the SEAK Writing Seminars, the creation of Steven Babitsky, Esq.

Jim Thayer and Amy Wallen are both accomplished writers and wonderful teachers, and they critiqued portions of my work at various stages of development. I thank them for their patience and apologize for any stubbornness.

My wife Theresa faithfully read the first draft of every chapter, providing important first blush commentary and continuing encouragement.

My daughter Deanna, a voracious reader and gifted writer, has great editing instincts. She is as adept at finding the dropped comma as she is at prescribing plot refinement. She made this a better story before it ever met the critical eye of an agent or editor.

Mary Jane Howell is the Public Relations Director for Dogwood Stable. She has been around thoroughbred horses all her life, and she knows the business inside out. She was my first pick for an insider review, and I'm grateful for her assistance.

Many other friends and associates were kind enough to read my story prior to publication, and each of them provided meaningful appraisal: Barry Roy, Paul, Nick and Joe Madelone, Dr. Bret Gelder and Dr. Agnes Gelder, Deborah Douglas, Bernard Conners, Dr. Robert Liebers and Dr. Susan DeLuke.

Special thanks to Gloria and Jocelyn Kelley of Kelley and Hall Book Publicity and to Monica Driver of Equus Media.

My father, Dr. Dominick DeLuke, smuggled me into Green Mountain Park to see my first horse race at the tender age of eleven, with a wink and a nod from the gate attendant—you had to be eighteen in those days at that particular race track. He later employed me on our farm in Chestertown, NY, during my high school and college years, at a time when he was a preeminent force in the breeding and the racing scene in New York, and I was just a college kid enjoying the horses.

W. Cothran Campbell is the founder of Dogwood Stable and the patriarch of the thoroughbred racing partnership. He has written three books on thoroughbred racing, chronicling a lifetime of people and places. His business model has been copied endlessly, but Cot continues to have that special knack for selecting a good horse at a moderate price. I've had the privilege of partnering on some of them.

Finally, for the cover, Barbara Livingston allowed me to use and modify her photo of Walsh, a Seattle Slew allowance horse, taken at trainer Pete Vestal's barn. Additionally, her photo of a morning workout in the mist at Saratoga was used for the title page. Barbara is an enormously talented equine photographer and a delightful person.

I have come to learn a great deal about the horses, the people, and the sport of thoroughbred racing over the years. It is a wonderful sport with a rich history, colorful characters, and at its epicenter, the magnificent thoroughbred racehorse.

"And of all the nonsensical things—I keep thinking about the horse!"

—Equus, Peter Shaffer

Prologue

The blindfold was torn off Dr. Gianni's eyes, and he squinted at the light, trying to focus on the two men who had dragged him from his office at gunpoint, thrown him into the back seat of a car, and transported him to the small room where he now sat. There were no windows, the only light coming from a bare bulb in a ceiling fixture. The walls were all cinder block, except for a metal garage door that had been closed behind them. The room seemed like part of a warehouse, or one of those self-storage units. With the blindfold off, Gianni could see a hint of sunlight where the cinder blocks abutted a tin roof.

Gianni was seated at a metal table, his hands bound behind his back. At one end of the table stood Sal Catroni. Unlike the other man, he wore no disguise. His longish hair was slicked back neatly, white at the sides, darker on top. His brow was furrowed in a scowl, amplifying the deep frown lines between his black-looking eyes.

Catroni spoke first. "You know who I am?" he said.

Gianni shook his head.

"I'm Sal Catroni, of the Catroni family, and this here is Hector. Hector was a medic in the marines. He's here to help you with some medical treatment."

Hector stood at least six-two, all of it solid muscle. He wore a tight white dress shirt, its silk sleeves rolled neatly to the middle of his massive forearms. A ski mask, open at the forehead, concealed his face, and his closely cropped black hair stood mostly on end. It reminded Gianni of a 1960s style flat-top cut, only not as stiff.

"Hector has some tools for you, Doc," Catroni said.

Hector opened a clean white linen cloth, the texture of a dishrag but with a starched white appearance. Inside were surgical instruments. Dr. Gianni instantly recognized them—there was a blade handle and several large #10 blades, the kind a surgeon would use to make a long incision. It was not a delicate blade, but one meant to cut hard and fast through a lot of tissue with a single swipe. Next to the blades was a bone cutting forceps, which Gianni knew to be a Rongeurs forceps. Then there was a large pile of neatly folded gauze pads.

"Recognize those tools?" Catroni asked.

Gianni nodded.

"Well, Hector here is prepared to do a little surgery today."

Catroni released Gianni's hands, placing his left hand on the table beside the white cloth, and the other hand behind Gianni's back, re-binding it tightly to the chair with duct tape.

"Now Dr. Gianni, Hector here is going to start with the tip of your ring finger, on your left hand. You are right-handed, aren't you?"

"What do you want from me?" Gianni said. He tried not to appear flustered. Years of surgical training and interminable hours on call had left him with a coolness under pressure, evident even now.

Catroni continued to talk. "It'll just be the tip, so he won't need that bone cutter, not right off anyway. And of course, we do have a few questions to ask you along the way, and maybe a favor or two, as well."

Hector struggled to put a pair of latex surgical gloves over his huge hands, then attached the blade to the handle with a dexterity that surprised Gianni, given the sheer size of his hands.

Hector said, "Hey, Sal, he's got no ring on it, no wedding band. You and Janice still married, Doc? Hold still, now, so I only take the tip."

Gianni thought the voice was vaguely familiar.

He used one hand to reinforce Catroni's grip on Gianni's left hand, isolating the finger and then slicing cleanly through the tip, taking less than an eighth of an inch with the blade cut. The cut was so fast that Gianni barely registered any pain, but he screamed, his sangfroid suddenly gone, when he saw Hector reach for the bone cutter.

"Relax," Hector said, "I just want to clip the nail end, so it's nice and neat. I want it to be nice and neat." He clipped the nail end square and flush with the amputated finger stump. Blood poured out from the cut skin and Gianni winced as Hector grabbed a clump of gauze and squeezed it over the bloody digit.

Catroni then untied Gianni's right hand, and Gianni instinctively clenched the blood drenched gauze in an attempt to slow the bleeding.

"Look," Hector said. "The doctor knows what to do for the bleeding."

Catroni spoke next. "Now you know that will heal just fine in no time. It was only a sliver, after all. And once it does, why, you'll be just as good a surgeon as you ever were, so we have no problem…yet.

But the problems will begin when Hector has to do more. Because the next cut is on the next finger over, the middle finger, and just a little farther up. So this time Hector gets to use that bone cutter to clip a little bone, too. Then it's on to the index finger, and a little higher up still. So by the time we get around to the thumb, the whole thing pretty much goes, Doc."

Chapter One

New York, NY

Dr. Anthony Gianni entered OR Suite 5 with his hands raised up as if in prayer, scrubbed and ready for the towel.

"Music to my ears," Dr. Larry Rosen said, stroking his salt and pepper goatee through his surgical mask.

"What's that?" asked Dr. Gianni.

"Regular sinus rhythm," Rosen said, looking up at the EKG machine. "It's music to my ears."

Rosen was not Gianni's favorite anesthesiologist, especially on a difficult case, though he was a damn good one and probably had an IQ that placed him in the upper echelons of Mensa. Gianni was perfectly comfortable with Larry's intelligence and clinical skills, it was just that the constant banter could wear on him after a while.

"You know what they say about anesthesia," Rosen continued, "Hours of boredom punctuated by moments of terror. I just love the boredom of that normal sinus rhythm: beep…beep…beep."

"Me, too." Over the years he had probably heard Larry profess that cliché no less than fifty times. He had also heard far too much about Rosen's computer whiz son, his shopaholic wife, and assorted gossip dealing with any of the OR staff who were fortunate enough to be in another room at that moment. Then, of course, there were countless jokes, mostly bad ones.

Gianni's hands were now dry and he thrust them one at a time into the gloves held by the scrub nurse.

"Anthony, how are your horses doing?" Rosen asked.

"Not now, Larry," Gianni said.

Rosen looked up at Gianni from his stool at the patient's head, then continued his banter. "All right, so listen to this joke, then. You hear the one about the definition of fascinate?"

"Don't think I have," Gianni said. "Can we put a CD in, Brenda?"

Brenda Byrne was functioning as the circulating nurse, coordinating the needs of the patient and the surgical team and working outside of the sterile field around the operating table. She answered in a husky voice that betrayed her long term smoking habit. "Sure, what do you have in mind?"

"Oh, I don't know…how about something classical to start with."

"Uggh," Rosen said, "Nothing worse than classical music at this hour of the morning."

"Too bad, Dr. Rosen," Brenda replied. "The surgeon is captain of the ship, you know."

"All right, so here's the story," Rosen went on undaunted.

Blue surgical drapes were placed over the patient, and the scrub nurse and surgical assistant took their positions around the operating table. Directly opposite Gianni was Dr. Willard Drew, who would act as first assistant on the case. Drew stood on a stool that boosted him eight inches. He remained quietly focused on the surgical site, now draped off and painted bright orange with betadyne, ready for the incision.

"Okay to begin?" Gianni asked.

"He's quiet as a puppy," Rosen said. "Go for it. Start time… 8:10 AM."

Gianni began with a single, smooth cut four inches in length. As blood oozed into the wound, Dr. Drew used the cautery to zap the bleeders.

"Great, Will, keep up with those."

"So these three kids are in their third grade class," Rosen started.

"Clamp, please." Dr. Drew continued to clamp off and cauterize the bleeders.

"And the teacher says, 'Who knows the definition of fascinate?' She says, 'You have to use the word properly in a sentence.'"

The surgeons were already through the skin and underlying structures, almost ready to expose the tumor in bone.

"The first kid says, 'I can do it…I can. When I see a bird fly, it fascinates me.' So the teacher says, 'That's good, Mary, that's good. Let's have another.'"

A Mozart piano concerto diluted Rosen's chatter, and Gianni spoke to Drew. "The tumor has broken through the bone right here, and based on the CT scan I think the margin of our resection should be over here."

"So the second kid says, 'The full moon in a clear sky is

fascinating.'"

"We're ready for the surgical saw now," Gianni said.

Rosen continued, "So then the third kid chimes in with his answer. 'Well, last Christmas we got this sweater for my Aunt Sharon. And it had twelve buttons. But she's so fat and her boobs are so big that she could only fasten eight.'"

Dr. Rosen let out a big belly laugh, but it was drowned out by the whine from the surgical saw as it cut through the diseased bone. Brenda and the scrub nurse groaned.

"You like that one, Anthony?"

"I think I heard it before," he said, passing the saw across to his assistant to complete the second cut, which would allow them to take out the tumor-filled bone and place a metal plate to bridge the defect.

Dr. Drew shifted his stance on the footstool and placed the saw tentatively. The beam from his headlight darted back and forth as he looked from the wound to the x-ray viewbox, then back again. "Here? What do you think, Anthony?"

"Well, you have to be sure you get all the diseased bone, so you have to be pretty high up, but we don't want to bag the maxillary artery. I can probably reach it from this side if you want, Will."

"No, I should do it, I've got a more direct line of vision on it."

Rosen stood up from his stool at the patient's head and peered into the surgical field. "Everything okay, boys?"

"Making good time," Gianni replied.

Drew began the cut and within seconds the entire field filled with bright red blood, as if a faucet had just been turned wide open. Drew froze.

Gianni spoke calmly but loudly now. "Two inch packing, lots of it and quickly please."

Drew recoiled somewhat unsurely, and Gianni spoke again. "There are four hands in this wound now, and they all need to be put to use. Will, suction." As quickly as he suctioned the field became completely filled with blood, the faucet still turned on full blast.

"Back to basics," Gianni said, "We pack the site and wait ten minutes."

Rosen looked at the suction canister filling with blood. "Okay, boys, from the looks of that canister we just lost about three units of blood. I'm calling for two units and some fresh frozen plasma. His pressure is down and we have a pulse of 130, sinus tach."

Blood continued to pour into the canister as Gianni packed several feet of gauze into the wound, like an accordion. It took several feet to completely pack the site. When the last of the gauze was pushed into the wound to tamponade the bleeding vessel, Gianni applied some hand pressure to the outer portion of the pack, and looked up at Drew.

After a few more minutes, Drew seemed to have regained his composure. He said, "The bleeding has slowed to a trickle, but we need to just sit tight for a few minutes now."

Gianni removed his hand from the top of the packing. "Ten more minutes by the clock," he said. "Countdown begins now, 8:40 a.m."

"Can't you clamp the damn thing?" Rosen asked.

Gianni loved it when the anesthesiologist suddenly became a surgeon. "Probably not, Larry. It's inaccessible to begin with, and it usually retracts up under the bone when it's cut. But with the pack we can stabilize things, and worst case scenario, we leave it in and return to the OR in forty-eight hours to remove it."

"Can you tie off the carotid?" Rosen asked.

"Won't help. Too much collateral flow from the opposite side of the neck."

"I once saw them tie off both sides," Rosen said.

Now Brenda apparently couldn't resist and added, "You can't do that because then the poor patient would end up with a brain like yours, Dr Rosen."

"Actually, it's the internal carotids that supply the brain," Gianni said. "But you've got a point there, Brenda, about Dr. Rosen I mean."

Once a cacophony of sound, the room was now silent. The operating room had no windows, and the only link to the outside world was an intercom on the one of the four white walls. The Mozart CD had ended but no one requested more music.

A man's voice on the intercom interrupted the silence. "Dr. Gianni, do you have a time estimate?"

"No I don't," Gianni said emphatically.

"Okay, just checking."

Rosen had hung the blood for transfusion, and it trickled into the patient's vein. The surgical pack was soaked bright red with blood, but no new blood appeared around the packing.

"This may just work, Will," Gianni said.

"I'm saying my prayers, that's about all we can do for the next few minutes," Drew said.

"We can at least have some music," Gianni said.

Brenda selected another classical piece, and this time Rosen kept his comments to himself. His eyes were fixed on the patient and on the suction canister. Chopin played in the background now, a nice selection, Gianni thought, serious but not too gloomy.

"Okay, Will, it's 8:52. What do you think?" The pack remained bright red, yet still, no new blood was evident around the margins of the pack.

"Gently we go…easy, easy," Gianni said. He grasped the end of the gauze packing with a forceps and pulled it slowly, straight out of the wound, carefully unwinding the folds of the accordion a few inches at a time. When the end was finally withdrawn, all eyes moved to the surgical site.

"Good," Gianni said. "It looks good. Let's just sit tight a little longer to make sure. And I'll need some Avitene hemostatic, several sheets, please."

After another few minutes of watchful waiting, Gianni and Drew were able to place a titanium plate to bridge the gap left after the tumor was excised. The wound was finally closed with a delicate, essentially invisible subcuticular stitch.

IT WAS 11:15 IN THE MORNING when Gianni returned to the surgeons' lounge. He had spoken with the patient's family after surgery, and he was slouched now in one of the well-worn lounge chairs, a bit worn himself for such an early hour. His day had really just begun. From the pocket of his scrub top he pulled out an index card that listed all of the calls he should be making today. The card was full, and the first three were all consulting physicians for some of his upcoming surgical cases next week. They could wait, as he didn't feel quite up to those in light of the earlier excitement. The fourth note, written in his own small script the night before, said "Call BRH." Bradford Randolph Hill. That was one he could readily handle right now. It would be a welcome diversion, they could talk about horses.

"Dr. Gianni calling for Mr. Hill, please."

"One moment."

"Anthony! Expected I might hear from you today."

"Listen, I was able to get Stu to meet you for dinner some night soon. You know he rarely does that much anymore, seems to have all the clients he needs, but he does want to meet you. I guess he likes what he's heard."

"Anthony, thank you, I really do appreciate that. Now which of the two-year-olds did you say you like?"

As Gianni spoke, he picked at a small hole in the arm of the upholstered chair. "Well, I've taken a twenty-five percent stake in Chiefly Endeavor. As far as I know, there is still at least one share left. So maybe we can have some fun with that one. Go to the Derby together, right?"

"Of course, isn't that what every owner of a reasonably bred two-year-old says?" Hill asked.

Gianni said, "An infamous Kentucky horseman once said, 'No one ever committed suicide with an untried two-year-old in the barn.'"

"I'll remember that."

Perhaps that line coined by the legendary Colonel Phil Chinn summed up the appeal of the thoroughbred game for Gianni— diversion, excitement, and potential, always lots of pure, unbridled potential. On this particular morning, it lightened the residual tension from the operating room.

Dr. Gianni quickly dressed and walked through the hospital corridor to his office in the adjacent Doctors' Pavilion. He had a long stride that made it difficult for others to keep up with him, and there was always a rhythmic bounce in his heels, causing his head to bob just slightly as he walked.

"IS HE HERE YET?" Janice Gianni shouted as she entered the reception area of her husband's plush Manhattan office. She was dressed in a leather mini skirt, Prada stiletto heels, and a tight blouse open well down her ample pectorals. She had a deeply tanned complexion and large brown eyes. Tiny gobs of mascara clung to her eyelids, and along with the dark shadow she had applied, seemed to spoil her natural beauty.

The receptionist finally recognized her as Dr. Gianni's wife, though she might as well have been the Strip-O-Gram girl who just wandered in the wrong door. "Well, he is *here*, but he is *very busy*."

"Not too busy for my anniversary surprise," Janice replied. "Five years today."

The two patients in the small waiting area looked up nervously from their magazines.

"I'm going back," she said, and in an instant she was through the closed door and into the treatment area.

Dr. Gianni stood outside one of the exam rooms, reviewing a chart. He looked up at her with a combination of anger and embarrassment on his face. "Janice? Why are you here? Dressed like...*that*?"

She flung her arms back, hitting one of the many elaborate diplomas adorning the hallway walls. "Happy Anniversary, baby!" she sang out, apparently oblivious, for the moment, to his dissatisfaction.

The past five years flashed before him, a kaleidoscope leaving him with the cold realization that, apart from some incredibly good sex, he had nothing in common with the woman before him. That was painfully clear to him now.

As Janice slowly read the expression on his face, her voluptuous smile faded to a frown, then to tears. She charged out the back door of the office, and Anthony retreated to his private office to collect himself yet again.

Chapter 2

Bradford Hill Jr. strode down the steps and into the foyer of Michael's Restaurant, glancing at his Patek Philippe watch. *6:30 p.m. Right on time.* Hill lived in a penthouse apartment on East 65th Street in Manhattan, and he owned a mansion on the water in Newport, Rhode Island, complete with fifty-two foot custom sailing vessel. The twenty-five years he'd spent in publishing had been good to him. A few of his friends owned racehorses, and the concept intrigued him. Dr. Gianni had told him about Bushmill Stable, and had arranged the meeting with Stuart Garrison Duncker, its venerable founder.

Michael's Restaurant was the media place to be, but Stuart Duncker would have much preferred the '21' Club, where he might have pointed out the Bushmill colors on the jockey at the entrance, or even Gallagher's, where his caricature was featured in the artist Peb's mural on the bar wall.

Hill turned to the small sitting area at the restaurant's entrance where a few leather chairs surrounded a table with an assortment of glossy magazines. Duncker put down his copy of *Hamptons* magazine. This was, coincidentally, one of Hill's publications, though Duncker didn't know it at the time, nor would he have particularly cared if he had.

"Mr. Duncker, this is a pleasure. Glad to see you found some good reading," he chortled with an artificial grin. The two men now stood face to face, their prominent chins pointed at one another. They peered with matching and slightly inauthentic smiles, more like fencing partners than new friends.

"Oh, yes," Duncker replied politely, "I did."

"Well, shall we be seated?"

Hill was dressed in a perfectly tailored, blue Brooks Brothers suit, club tie, expensive loafers. Duncker had settled on a blazer and his version of the club tie featuring the blue and white racing silks of Bushmill Stable.

Both men looked tanned and fit. They were escorted to a quiet table near the far wall, just as Hill had requested. He sat first, facing the crowd, and then invited Duncker to sit opposite him.

The waiter appeared seconds later. "May I offer you gentlemen a drink?"

Hill smiled with recognition at the waiter and said, "I'll have a Bombay Martini, extra, *extra* dry, three olives."

"And you, sir?"

Duncker replied in a smooth southern drawl, "Iced tea for me, please." He made no secret of the fact that he was a recovering alcoholic and hadn't consumed a drink in over thirty years. Duncker had also given up the courtship of new clients long ago. The reputation of Bushmill Stable was such that he was no longer required to do it. He was blessed with plenty of clients who were more than willing to risk considerable cash on the hope and promise of a great thoroughbred. He had agreed to this meeting only because he had to be in Manhattan anyway, and Dr. Gianni had asked him to meet with Hill.

Hill asked, "So which of those two-year-olds do you like the best?" All prospective new clients and even some old ones couldn't resist asking that one question, which in Duncker's mind was akin to asking, "Who's your favorite child?"

Duncker continued in his slow southern drawl, "Why I like them all, Bradford, otherwise I wouldn't have bought them. But I will say that I am particularly fond of Chiefly Endeavor. He is by one of this year's leading stallions, Dynaformer. The dam is a stakes winner herself, and her first two foals are both winners too. Hard to beat that at his sale price. This is her *third* foal, of course. He's a real bruiser, stands about sixteen-three and has the bone, muscle and physique to go with it. Intelligent look to him, could be a *real good one*." The last three words were drawn out in slow southern longhand. "But in this business there are no guarantees. I *always* tell my clients that I don't want to see a penny that you can't afford to lose, and I absolutely mean that." That was Duncker's standard approach with clients—brutally honest, always with the highest hope, but low expectations.

"Count me in on a share in Chiefly Endeavor. I've studied the material, and of course, I place a good deal of trust in the opinion of our mutual friend, Dr. Gianni. I guess I just needed to meet the patriarch of Bushmill Stable myself, and now that I have, well as I said, count me in on Chiefly Endeavor."

"I most certainly will and we are delighted to have you with us." Even though Duncker was no longer courting clients, he was happy to have another from "the grid." He often analyzed the demographics of his client base, rating their desirability. Manhattan's grid, or the areas represented by zip codes 10021 and 10028, was among the best. He had many clients from the publishing industry, also a generally desirable bunch. Doctors were among the worst. They seemed to want to dissect every last detail of a pedigree or a billing statement. It was a wonder Gianni had lasted as long as he had with Bushmill. Duncker and Gianni did genuinely like and respect one another, nonetheless.

Brad Hill, on the other hand, had just spent $75,000 for a twenty-five percent stake in a massive but fragile four-legged athlete, sight unseen, in the time it had taken for his cocktail to arrive.

Chapter 3

Saratoga Springs, NY
Three months later

The rising sun had begun to penetrate the thick fog overlying the famed Oklahoma training track in Saratoga Springs. *Like the pea soup over the New England coast,* Gianni thought as he approached the gate on Union Avenue, drove inside and headed towards the training track. The fog over the track reminded him of the still fog over a harbor, blurring the shapes of horses rather than boats, of jockeys not sailors. *Fog so thick it feels like a misting rain when you walk through it.*

Gianni loved the early morning tranquility of both scenes, though of late he had abandoned the seascapes in favor of the training track. Once inside those gates, he felt as though he were a million miles from the hustle of Manhattan and the frenzy of a big city emergency room.

THE WORLD INSIDE the gates of the Oklahoma Track usually exploded with activity around mid July, though it remained open from spring through late autumn. Saratoga was the venue where all owners and trainers wanted to spend the summer, hoping they had the sort of stock to compete against the best in the world.

Brad Hill was already parked along the track, chatting with another owner when Gianni drove by. "Good morning, Mr. Hill. Hop in and I'll drive you to the barn."

"Perfect vehicle for this place, Anthony," Hill said as he opened the door of the black Jeep Wrangler.

Gianni said, "Hold on. It's not the ride you're accustomed to in your Range Rover."

They rocked up and down over ruts in the dirt road and pulled up on the grass across from Barn 74, Jeff Willard's barn.

"He's been training really well," Gianni said. "Jeff thinks he could be ready in August, September for sure. Though nothing is really for sure where thoroughbreds are concerned. If nothing else, Brad, horses will save you from a predictable life."

They parked on a grassy area in front of the shedrow, a row of a dozen or so individual stalls facing a walkway. The smell of hay and manure was unmistakable when they approached the barn.

Most of the trainers converted the end stalls to offices. As they walked towards Jeff's office at the end of the barn, Gianni recognized their horse heading at them.

"Look, here he comes now, right on schedule."

"Good looking animal," Hill said. "I'd love to see him make his debut while we're still in Saratoga."

"Wouldn't we all."

Chiefly Endeavor was slotted for one of the earlier sets, and the muscular colt was now prancing sideways, full of himself, with

Alison McKensie in the saddle. Alison was one of Jeff's strongest exercise riders, and she had taken a special interest in the Chief, her nickname for the fractious two-year-old. Her legs were covered by leather chaps that hugged the barrel of the horse, and her blond hair was tied in a long pony tail that wagged behind her safety helmet, nearly in unison with the horse's tail.

"Come on," Gianni said. "Let's go watch from the viewing stand." They changed direction and walked back across a grassy area to the training track.

At every barn there were grooms tending to horses in the stalls, hot walkers circling them around the shedrows after their workouts, and exercise riders up and down on horses in a continual parade to and from the track. Trainers walked from the barn to the track and back again, on foot or on horseback, stopping to exchange words with anxious owners who always had questions for which there were often no answers.

From a host of illegals just up from Mexico, to the likes of the Whitneys and the Vanderbilts, the world inside the gates was a microcosm of the world outside. Even the horses exhibited a class system. Each barn had its alpha male, with others assuming more submissive roles, not unlike a litter of dogs. Among the two-year-olds in Jeff Willard's barn, word was spreading that Chiefly Endeavor was the new alpha-elect.

Gianni could see Jeff standing in front of the viewing stand, a small bleacher-like structure raised several feet above ground level. At six-foot-three, Jeff could forego the stand. He looked back and forth between the stopwatch in his hand and his horse on the track.

"Four furlongs in forty-nine and one. Not bad, not bad," he said.

"Good morning, Jeff."

"Morning, Doc. Your colt is next."

"Jeff, meet Brad Hill." They exchanged pleasantries, and then the three climbed the stairs of the viewing stand.

"He'll be going five furlongs on the turf."

The fog had lifted, and the trio had a clear view across the track to the far side of the turf course. At the five-eighths marker they could see Chiefly Endeavor accelerate.

"Good stride," Jeff said. "Look at the way he holds his head, he's fluid and he has a good long stride. That's a good horse."

As he crossed in front of the finish pole, Jeff clicked his timer. "Looks like 1:02 flat, without looking like he had to work all that hard. That's good." Jeff began to walk back towards his barn with Gianni and Brad Hill at his side.

Jeff said, "Doc, I was going to call you this morning. Chiefly Endeavor is our good news of the day, but I'm afraid I have some bad news as well. The filly got very sick yesterday."

Gianni only had one filly, so he knew Jeff was referring to his three-year-old, a pretty chestnut named Boots. "What's wrong with her?"

"After that last race, when she ran so poorly, I thought she might have a laryngeal paralysis. The jockey said she seemed to just quit, and she was blowing hard like she couldn't get air."

"The vet was going to look at her next week, right?"

"Yeah, and in the meantime she started to drain this foul smelling mucus out of her nose, on one side only. The vet scoped her and at first he thought it was a tumor. Then on closer examination, he found and removed a sponge."

"A what?"

"A sponge," Jeff replied.

"How the hell did a sponge get in her nose?"

"You've never heard or read anything about sponging?"

Gianni stopped walking and looked quizzically at the trainer, then at Hill.

Jeff continued, "Sponging. A piece of sponge is inserted deep into one of the nostrils. It interferes with breathing, and obviously with the horse's ability to run. Longer term, it will cause infection and a whole host of problems if it's not found in time."

"My God, who would do that to a horse?" Hill asked.

"Hard core gamblers, organized crime, crooked trainers or owners," Jeff said.

Gianni shook his head in disgust. "I want to see her."

"In her case, I can't figure any motive," Jeff said. "That race was a low level claiming race, so an owner or trainer would have to be pretty desperate for a lousy win. And she wasn't enough of a threat in that race for some high stakes gambler to target her and try to put her out of the running. In fact, the favorite won that race and paid peanuts. Right now it's in the hands of the police and the Racing and Wagering Board."

"Can I see her now?" Gianni asked again.

"Sure, she's lying down in her usual stall. The vet thinks she'll be okay. One more thing, though." Jeff stopped walking and gave a somber look in Gianni's direction. "She's the third horse this month who was sponged right here in the backstretch at Saratoga."

Bradford Hill looked quizzically at the trainer, then at Gianni. "What kind of business have I gotten myself into, Anthony?"

Chapter Four

Armonk, NY

"Must you drink that now, Janice?" Gianni said.

She looked up at her husband with a bored expression on her face. "It's only water."

"The hell it is, and Jesus Christ, it's not even noon yet."

Janice took a generous gulp of the clear iced liquid, then clinked the glass loudly on the table beside her. "Come here and taste it if you don't believe me."

"I don't have to. I can tell by the way you swig it. Christ, I didn't even have to come out here to know. I can tell by the way you clink the goddamn glass on the table. I can hear it from upstairs."

Janice smiled, replaced her sunglasses, laid back in the recliner and stared at the sun. She had recently bleached her hair blonde, and she twirled the streaks idly with her fingers.

"I'm not going to argue today, we have to be at Belmont for the fifth race," he said.

"I know, I just want to get a little more sun," she said.

"And I want to leave here by one-thirty at the latest. Aren't you tan enough already? It's almost time to close the pool for God's sake. Another week and it'll be full of leaves."

"Never tan enough. I want to look as tan as your friend Brad Hill does today."

"One-thirty, Janice. And if you're not ready I'm leaving without you."

They left together at one-thirty-five. Janice had finished a second tumbler of vodka and was considerably more chatty now.

When they arrived at the track, she lagged behind her husband as she struggled to navigate the soft gravel walkways in her four inch heels. Gianni made little effort to alter the pace for her. He hustled his way past the attendant at the entrance to the paddock, a brief wave exchanged between them.

A towering white pine tree sat in the center of the paddock, its many branches reaching out like huge tentacles at all angles, some skyward, others growing out horizontally from the fat trunk. In an area outside the shade of the great pine, a bronze statue of Secretariat glinted in the sunlight, giving tribute to the horse's spectacular thirty-one length romp in the 1973 Belmont Stakes and his capture of the Triple Crown.

Gianni went directly to stall four, where he met up with Jeff Willard. A double-breasted, light grey suit framed the trainer's tall, rugged body. His boyish face and blue eyes appeared a bit incongruous, belonging on a smaller frame, perhaps. Jeff wasn't always the most winning trainer, but he usually found himself ranked in the top fifty nationwide. More importantly, Gianni knew that Jeff understood how to treat horses. Often quoting one of his mentors, Jeff would remind his owners that "if you take good care of the horses, they'll take good care of you."

"How's he looking, Jeff?"

"He's fit, Doc. Mean as hell like the old man, but fit. Tried to bite the blacksmith again this week."

Gianni looked devotedly at the animal. Chiefly Endeavor was large for a two-year-old, a dark brown muscular animal with an alert demeanor and an intelligent look in his eye. He reared slightly and shifted his body when the saddle was cinched up under his flank, then again after his tongue was secured with a thick elastic band to keep it from interfering with his airway—a technique many trainers utilize before a race.

Chief pranced off alertly to join the other two-year-olds in the paddock. There were seven other horses, and nearly in unison eight jockeys got the "leg up" as they were boosted like anxious little warriors into the irons.

Anthony was rejoined by Janice, who had found Brad Hill on the way in, and the two had been quite content to gab and watch the people in the paddock while Anthony tended to the horse. Alison McKensie, the exercise rider, was there too. She could have easily passed for one of the owners, wearing a simple but elegant print dress that accentuated her shapely torso and muscular calves, conditioned by years on horseback.

Together they all followed Jeff out of the paddock area. They walked by a block of betting windows, where edgy bettors lined up ten deep. Some carried crumpled *Racing Forms* and scribbled combinations of numbers with pen or pencil as they nudged their way forward in line.

"How do we get to the winner's circle from here?" Alison asked.

"Jeff knows," Gianni said.

Hill and Janice continued their chitchat as they walked behind the rest of the group, following them to Bushmill Stable's box on the third level of the clubhouse. Janice took one of the corner seats, and everyone else stood in front of their seats and looked over the crowd to the track below.

The track announcer had begun to introduce the eight horses as they pranced towards the grandstand for the post parade:

NUMBER FOUR IS CHIEFLY ENDEAVOR, OWNED BY BUSHMILL STABLE, TRAINED BY JEFF WILLARD AND RIDDEN BY RAFAEL BEJARANO.

Anthony glanced down at his program. *Race 5, For Maidens, Two Years Old, One Mile on the Turf.* Then under his horse, *Chiefly Endeavor, by Dynaformer, out of Still Mine.* He didn't look at any of the other entries, though he had studied them earlier. He knew that he was in a race with some famous owners, the sheiks and the Kentucky blue bloods. Racing may be the sport of kings but it can also be a great equalizer at times. Funny Cide had proven that. Six buddies from western New York purchased that seemingly ordinary gelding for $75,000 as a two-year-old. Funny Cide went on to win the Kentucky Derby and the Preakness, and to bankroll $3.5 million in earnings.

Anthony looked through his binoculars as the horses were nearing the starting gate. The track at Belmont Park is a mile and a half long, so for this one mile race on the turf the horses would start at the farthest end, across the track from the clubhouse, and would go through only one full turn before their run to the finish line. Many of the two-year-olds were skittish and took a long time to enter the gate. Chiefly Endeavor was one of the last to enter, but he went right in and stood like a pro his first time out. The announcer began his call of the race:

THEY'RE IN THE GATE…AND THEY'RE OFF. FAST FALL AND PHONE TAG SHOW EARLY SPEED, FOLLOWED BY ATONED AND THE EDITOR. THEN IT'S A GAP OF THREE LENGTHS BACK TO KID ROW AND ELECTRIFY IS SIXTH. CHIEFLY ENDEAVOR IS SEVENTH, SAVING GROUND ALONG THE RAIL, AND THE TRAILER IS WALL STREET SCANDAL. THE FIRST QUARTER WENT IN 23 AND 2, AN HONEST PACE FOR THESE TURF MAIDENS…

"It's okay," Jeff said, "I like him where he is now. The pace is strong. He's good."

…AND THE HALF WENT IN 46 AND 1, WITH FAST FALL CONTINUING TO SET A VERY HEALTHY PACE FOR THIS FIELD OF JUVENILES.

Gianni continued to listen to the track announcer as he focused on the royal blue Bushmill colors through his binoculars.

AND IT IS WIDE OPEN NOW…CHIEFLY ENDEAVOR IS SUDDENLY THIRD AND LOOKING FOR ROOM ON THE INSIDE BUT CAN'T FIND IT… KID ROW HAS NOW TAKEN THE LEAD FROM FAST FALL, BUT WITH A BLANKET OF HORSES NOW CHASING FOR THE LEAD, AS THE FIELD TURNS FOR HOME.

Through his binoculars, Anthony saw the jockey tap his horse left-handed, causing him to veer to the outside where he found room to race towards the front runners.

NOW NEARING THE FINAL SIXTEENTH, KID ROW AND FAST FALL CONTINUE TO VIE FOR THE LEAD, AND NOW CHIEFLY ENDEAVOR IS CHARGING WITH A LATE MOVE ON THE OUTSIDE…CHIEFLY ENDEAVOR HAS TAKEN THE LEAD NOW BY TWO LENGTHS AND

AS THEY CROSS THE WIRE IT IS CHIEFLY ENDEAVOR BY AN
INCREASING FIVE LENGTHS. THE MILE ON THE TURF WENT IN
134 AND 2, A VERY IMPRESSIVE SHOWING FOR CHIEFLY
ENDEAVOR OVER THIS TALENTED FIELD OF MAIDEN TWO-
YEAR-OLD TURF RUNNERS.

Alison was jumping up and down, Jeff's fist pumped the air
in front of him, and Dr. Gianni, while composed as usual, felt as
though his heart might jump out of his chest. He gave Brad a hearty
handshake. Janice was still seated, and Gianni leaned over to kiss his
wife on the cheek.

"See, Anthony, things really are looking up," Janice said.

Chapter 5

The middle-aged lady wore rose colored glasses, and she was lying flat on the operating table. They were safety glasses and they were part of the protocol for any patient having laser surgery. Tufts of bleached red hair poked out along the edges of her surgical cap.

In his hand, Dr. Gianni held a black, pencil-sized instrument attached via a flexible black wire to a carbon dioxide laser machine. The machine looked like a large robot, a tall white structure on wheels, with a confusing array of touch buttons and digital gauges. Each time he activated the laser, it made a clicking sound and emitted an invisible beam of light energy, vaporizing the brown spots on her face.

"Do you use the same machine for wrinkles?" the patient asked.

"Well, the same machine, used in a somewhat different manner than for the solar keratosis areas," Gianni said.

He studied the numerous wrinkles on her face and neck, some fine and narrow, others deep and crevicular. Like the brown spots he was treating, they were all aggravated by years of sun exposure compounded by years of smoking. He imagined for a moment, *this is how Janice will look in fifteen years. Maybe less if she doesn't lay off the cigarettes and booze, and cut her sun exposure by about eighty percent. Her fondness for all three seemed to be increasing, though she hadn't always been that way.*

"I guess I should have thought of that at the consultation appointment," she said. "Too late now, right?"

"There is a distinct protocol that we follow, but we can go through it at another appointment if you think you may want to know more about that particular surgery."

The last of the brown spots was transformed into an ash-like eschar.

"Now these areas are going to look worse for a while before they look better. We're going to review some instructions with you, but I want to emphasize that you must stay out of the sun for a while. Expect the areas to look a little pink or reddish. That will go away, but the after care is extremely important. Any questions?"

Gianni noticed his receptionist standing at the doorway to the operatory. He stepped outside the door and she said quietly, "Mr. Duncker is on the phone. Will you take it or should I take a message?"

"Tell him I'm just finishing a case, but I'll be with him in a minute," he said quietly. Gianni peeked back in to finish speaking with his patient, then walked to his private office, closed the door and grabbed the phone. "Good morning, Stu."

"Well good morning to you, Anthony. That colt of ours was certainly *impressive* his first time out. I'm glad you were able to be there, and we'll send you the photo from the winner's circle."

"That was a thrill, I must say."

"And we are *thrilled* with his performance. His jockey said he barely asked him the question in the stretch, and you saw how he responded. Quite a turn of foot, I must say. So we're looking to enter him in a *stake* next. Maybe the Pilgrim Stakes back at Belmont. Only thing, that one comes up pretty soon. And he did have a little bleeding from his lungs after that first race, so we'll up his lasix a little next time and I expect we'll just *let the horse* tell us when he's ready to run again."

"Bleeding? Has he ever shown blood before?" Gianni asked.

"Once after a hard work on dirt, Jeff tells me, though he generally seems to do quite well on grass."

"Well, I'm all for letting the horse tell us when he's ready. Let's not push him too much, right?" Gianni said.

"Right you are, my friend. We'll be in touch, okay?"

"Right, one more thing though. How's the filly doing?" Gianni said.

"Oh, Boots. She's fine. Recovered completely from that sponging episode, thank God. Still no leads on who was behind it, I'm afraid."

Chapter 6

Gianni left the Diplomat Hotel in the late afternoon. The convertible top was down and the day was unusually hot for January in Miami. The smell of ocean salt was pleasant and strong as he headed south on Ocean Drive toward Hallandale Boulevard, then on to Gulfstream Park.

He put a CD in the player. The first selection to play was from *Phantom of the Opera*.

As he listened to the lyrics, he somehow knew that a victory loomed.

Approaching the entrance to the track, Gianni was unnerved. Where he remembered a low profile clubhouse, he now saw a rather gaudy assortment of buildings, some a few stories tall, some higher. *Frank's idea of progress, I guess*, Gianni thought, referring to the track's current owner. It looked more like a casino, less like the old racetrack he remembered.

Actually, it was because of Frank's seemingly misguided attempts at expansion that Gulfstream was even open this early, and for that, Gianni was happy. *Better a fresh turf course near the season opener than the well-worn and rough course at Calder Racetrack's closing.*

He went directly to the paddock, arriving just in time to meet Chiefly Endeavor's other connections. As he walked, he looked down at the mass of synthetic pavers that lined the entire walking arena. Not a single patch of living grass had survived the renovation.

Jeff Willard had just saddled the horse, and he reached down to slip off the protective bell boots, extending and then stretching each of the front legs in the process. From the hind legs, a groom spun off two bandages with amazing speed and handwork.

"Anthony, I was afraid you might not make it," Stu Duncker said, extending his hand. "Where's Janice?"

"Business at home," Gianni said. "She couldn't make it."

Duncker shifted his beige Stetson dress hat a tad and said, "Well, she may miss a trip to the winner's circle."

"We're certainly in good company, I didn't know Her Majesty the Queen was expected to have an entry. I don't imagine she made the trip from England for our little stakes race, did she?"

"You'll only see that for the rare Triple Crown race," Duncker replied with his southern drawl. "Not that a Grade II on the turf is anything to scoff at. Remind me after the race and I'll tell you a little historical tale from *across the pond*. It has to do with Chiefly's great, great, great grand sire, a horse named Royal Charger, in the Queen Anne Stakes of 1945. It was the event that got me hooked on this crazy business. I'll recount it later—the horses are about to leave the paddock. It's a splendid bit of racing history, really."

RIDERS UP.

"We have a table on level three," Duncker said. "Not the best *view* through the glass enclosure up there. I think they've ruined this place in the name of progress. The paddock is an abomination. It certainly wasn't designed *with the horses* in mind."

"Actually, I'm going to just jockey for position at the rail. I'll be near the winner's circle, and I'll be where I can hear the hoofs pound the turf as they head for home."

"Good man, I like your spirit," Duncker said. "See you in the winner's circle."

The view from the rail was still pleasant enough. Palm trees and a line of tall buildings off in the horizon provided a familiar, pacific backdrop. The hoof beats were still thunderous as the horses turned for home. The bright and myriad colors of the silks against the green turf course were spectacular. Reds, greens, yellows, and as the horses entered the stretch run, Bushmill's royal blue and white, moving along the outside and approaching the two leaders. Only the width of the outer dirt track separated Gianni from the horses and he could hear the cajoles of the jockeys, yelling at their horses and each other. Once they flew by, he had to turn his focus to the announcer to hear the finish.

AND THEY'RE DOWN TO THE FINAL FURLONG AND IT'S CHAKOS AND CHIEFLY ENDEAVOR. CHIEFLY ENDEAVOR COMING AT CHAKOS. FIFTY YARDS FROM HOME...CHIEFY ENDEAVOR AND CHAKOS...CHAKOS AND CHIEFLY ENDEAVOR...AND CHIEFLY ENDEAVOR NAILS HIM, TO TAKE THE GRADE II TROPICAL STAKES IN 1:32 and 1, A VERY FAST MILE HERE AT GULFSTREAM PARK, AND CLOSE TO THE STAKES RECORD.

I felt it, I knew it, Gianni thought. He put his binoculars back into their carrying case and hustled his way through the crowd to the winner's circle. Jeff Willard and Duncker arrived, and all eyes were on Chiefly Endeavor as he jogged down the track and pranced into the circle. He looked strong and not nearly as lathered up as some of the other horses.

"The way he galloped out, I think he could have easily gone another furlong or two," Jeff commented.

After their picture was taken with the horse and jockey, the group left the winner's circle and stood alongside the paddock. Artificial fountains in the center of the paddock gushed spouts of water and the wind carried a fine, cooling mist in their direction. Duncker began to recount the story of Royal Charger.

"I was basically a kid and had just finished my time in the Navy, looking to find my way in the world. Those were the war years, of course, so there was little or no racing in the states. My uncle was a racing fan and a very well-connected fellow. He had taken me under his wing and I had the privilege of going with him to this most prestigious race at the Ascot Racecourse. The dress code during the meet required morning coats and top hats for men, and formal dresses and hats for ladies. That dress code stands to this day. Anyway, my uncle had arranged everything, and I was quite taken by the whole affair. The pageantry, the beautiful turf course, lots of attractive ladies, and some of the best racehorses in the world."

Gianni looked attentively at Duncker as he continued his story.

"I had always loved horses, but now I was hooked. My uncle later employed me in his advertising agency. I stayed with that until I had enough money and enough courage to pursue racing full time and to ultimately start Bushmill. The horse that won the Queen Anne

Stakes that day was a horse called Royal Charger. That horse, Anthony, was the great, great, great grand sire of Chiefly Endeavor."

"The pedigrees are one of the things I enjoy most about this business," Gianni said. "And of course, the marvelous animals themselves. Now, Chief's grass pedigree comes from the top line primarily, right?"

"Right. Although Dynaformer, as I'm sure you know, can run on dirt as well. In fact, we need to start thinking about that relative to his next race. If he can do on dirt close to what he does on grass, then we could potentially have a horse on the Derby trail."

"You really think so?"

"I'd like to try him at a mile and a sixteenth or a mile and an eighth on dirt. More on that later. Will you join us for dinner, Anthony? We're going to Joe's Stone Crab."

"I'd love to if there's room."

"I'm here alone so it will just be the two of us and Greg Jacobs, our Ocala trainer and his wife. I'm sure you'd enjoy speaking with them."

GIANNI DIALED his wife's cell phone as he left Gulfstream Park.

"Did you see the race?"

"I had to show some houses. About all I could do was look at the chart online from my office. It was a close one, huh?"

"Did you tape it at least?" Anthony asked.

"I couldn't, Anthony."

"You could have used the timer. Well, I'll get the stakes tape from the track. A grade II win second time out—I want that one for my collection. Is someone in the car with you, Janice?"

"No, it's a CD."

"It sounds like someone yelling."

"RULE NUMBER 14: ORIGINALITY CAN BE DANGEROUS. YES, ORIGINALITY MAY ACTUALLY BE DANGEROUS."

"It's called Gorilla Marketing. It has some great ideas for promoting my real estate sales."

"Oh."

Gianni turned on the CD player in his rental car. The tape of theatre selections was still in the deck. A tune from *Song and Dance* played.

> *Don't want to know who's to blame*
> *It won't help knowing*
> *Don't want to fight day and night*

The tape also continued in Janice's Mercedes:

"WEAPON # 16: DIRECT MAIL LETTERS. THIS POWERFUL TOOL..."

"Can you hear me, Janice?"

"Yeah, but it sounds like you're in a wind tunnel."

"I have the top down and some music on."

"Where are you anyway?"

"I'm headed south on Collins Ave. I'm meeting a few people for dinner at Joe's Stone Crabs."

"Nice."

"You could have come, Janice."

"RULE 19: IDENTIFY AND CREATE YOUR COMPETITIVE ADVANTAGE."

"Well, I didn't. When are you coming back?"

Don't run off in the pouring rain

"My flight is due in around 5:30 Sunday."

"I'll see you then," she said.

"WEAPON NUMBER 21: FAX ON DEMAND..."

Take the hurt out of all the pain...

Tell me on a Sunday please...

"Bye."

Chapter 7

The security gate at Palm Beach Downs requires a code to be entered onto a keypad, but the code is posted in the window of the unmanned gate house. In years gone by, there must have been some need for a higher level of security. Now, most of the trainers who stabled horses at the training center preferred the low key feeling, much quieter than the larger and more modern Palm Meadows, just one exit up the Florida Turnpike.

Gianni drove through the gate and down the dirt road that led past the training track, a mile-long oval with a pond in the center of the track. On the opposite side of the road were six barns, all painted pale yellow with maroon-colored tin roofs. Gianni pulled up to the second building and parked alongside a row of four palm trees that bordered the end of the barn.

GIANNI WAS A FREQUENT visitor to the barn the morning after a race, and he was surprised to see Stu Duncker there when he drove up to Willard's barn. Unlike Gianni, Stu rarely saw his horse except on a race day. He was accompanied today by a large man, at least six feet tall with a round belly spilling through the suspenders that held up his chino work pants. He had a balding head, a rotund and ruddy face and a generally odious demeanor.

"Morning, Anthony," Duncker said. "I have someone I would like you to meet. This is Chester Pawlek. Chester, meet Dr. Anthony Gianni."

The big man had a pronounced stutter, not consistent, but awkward when it appeared. "Stu tells me you're one of the best s-s-surgeons in New York City."

"Stu is very kind," Gianni said.

"Chester is in the construction business in New Jersey," Duncker said, "and he has a growing stable of thoroughbreds. He's bought some damn good ones in New York, as well as in Florida and Kentucky."

They were standing in the shedrow. In one of the stalls, a groom held a horse's halter while a blacksmith braced the horse's foot in a hoof jack and nailed a shoe into place with a rhythmic "whack, whack, whack."

Alison McKensie emerged next from a stall further down the shedrow. "Congratulations, Dr. Gianni," she said. "How about our boy there!"

"Fantastic, Alison, and due in large part to your hard work in the morning."

"I love that horse," she said, "though I must say, the older he gets the harder he is to handle. Do you know we only have one groom who will go into the stall with him?"

Stu and Chet walked off across a grassy area in the direction of the training track. Alison raised her chin toward the large man. "Get a load of him," she said.

Gianni took a bag of carrot pieces he had brought and offered a piece at a time to Chiefly Endeavor. The horse took each piece from the palm of Gianni's hand, crunching and swallowing a few pieces at a time, then following each swallow with a grunt and a strong pull on the nylon covered chain that stretched across the top of his stall door. When he grabbed the chain with his mammoth teeth, the whole door shook and the chain clanged.

"What do you mean?" Gianni asked.

"The fat guy," she replied. "I heard them talking to Jeff earlier. He wants to buy a majority interest in the horse, and he was throwing some pretty big numbers around. I don't know, Doc. I just get bad vibes from the guy."

Chiefly Endeavor stretched his neck out of the stall, then turned his head to the side, as if imploring for more carrots. Gianni obliged.

"Well, my share's not for sale. It doesn't matter what the offer is."

"I know that. You're the only partner I've actually seen around the barn. Anyway, go in Jeff's office and look at the photo of yesterday's win in the *Daily Racing Form*. It's a great shot."

"I'll take a look right now."

"And I have to keep moving, Doc. Lots to do yet."

"I know, don't let me hold you up."

She yelled something in Spanish to one of the hotwalkers, and the fellow ran off into one of the stalls. One of the other Hispanic men taunted the first, yelling "*Corra, corra.*"

"*Usted tambien,*" Alison yelled.

The first fellow howled.

Gianni was increasingly curious about Chester. He had thought him to be rather unctuous after their brief exchange. He walked over to join the two men along the rail of the training track. On his way, he passed a young boy playing with a dump truck in the dirt. The boy made a groaning sound, imitating the roar of a truck as he moved his toy across the ground.

On the track, horses went by, some in a slow gallop, others breezing for the clocker. Chester stood at the rail next to the eighth pole, a distance marker with black and white horizontal stripes, topped off by a cast iron horse head. Chet's ample belly hung over the top of the metal railing and his large, red hands gripped it tightly.

Duncker said, "Anthony, Chester has expressed interest in buying into Chiefly Endeavor, and of course I am obligated to present the offer to each of the partners. He has offered $750,000 for any of the partners who agree to sell their one-quarter ownership interest. Bushmill will of course remain as the managing partner per the original contract. I will offer no opinion as to what a partner should do, though I am always happy to see a share price appreciate ten times in less than a year. I would have called you tomorrow, but since we are all here, I thought I would present the offer and I can follow up tomorrow. So you'll have a little time to mull it over."

"I won't need any time. My share is not for sale."

"I somehow expected you might say that," Duncker said. "They tell me you've become quite attached to that colt."

Chester lumbered off across the lawn without a word.

STU DUNCKER SUBSEQUENTLY presented the same offer to Brad Hill and the other two partners. Hill refused but each of the other two accepted Chester's offer. The two partners who accepted the offer were provided a handsome return on their original $75,000 investment. It also provided Chester with fifty-percent ownership in Chiefly Endeavor, and it meant that Gianni would have to spend more time around Chester Pawlek.

Chapter 8

"Dr. Gianni, you have a call from the ER on line two, Dr. Moravic." He thought he had finished with patients for the day and sitting at his desk, was about to begin reviewing his mail.

"Hello Stan, what surprise do you have in store for me this evening?"

"We've got a pretty nasty injury. Forty-two year old male found himself on the wrong end of a machete. Probably some sort of mob war deal. Anyway, he is conscious, alert, and there don't appear to be any other injuries. But his face is literally filleted open from an area just below and well lateral to the eye, extending down below the border of the mandible. The laceration is at least 12 centimeters, probably longer. The most amazing thing is that the blade went cleanly through and also split the jaw bone apart in a saggital plane. You see it on the PA view of the skull. The whole cut looks like it was done with almost surgical precision."

"Is the bleeding controlled?'

"We packed the wound with gauze. There's no active bleeding now."

"How about the facial nerve?"

"Grossly intact. I think the cut was far enough distal so that most of the branches were spared. I might have noted just a slight weakness when he closed his eyes tightly. I'm sure you'll be a better judge of that. All in all, I'd say he's one lucky bastard. I don't know what the attacker was aiming for, but he managed to miss all the vital structures."

"Have the police been there?"

"Yeah, but the guy's not talking. Naturally he was just minding his own business, didn't know the attacker, and blah blah. But the police know the guy and he clearly has some mob ties. He's actually a rather likable sort, well-mannered in a tough guy way."

"I assume the plastics resident has evaluated him?"

"That's another issue, Anthony. We were paging him for at least a half hour before we called you."

"Jesus Christ, who's on?"

"The senior resident on call is Matt Kantor. The first year guy has been totally swamped doing minor stuff in the ER at the County."

"Have them keep trying Kantor, will you please. What the hell is it with these guys anyway?"

"This isn't the first time for him, I guarantee that."

"I'll be in shortly."

Matt Kantor eventually answered his page and prepared the patient for the OR. The injury was too extensive to repair in the emergency room, but it needed to be repaired as soon as possible.

Both the resident and the attending anesthesiologist were there when Gianni and Kantor entered the surgeons' dressing room. Kantor was a short, stocky Korean lad who had been adopted as an infant and brought from Seoul to the United States. His parents were wealthy New Yorkers who had no other children and probably coddled the youth from infancy, Gianni thought.

Larry Rosen was the attending on call, and he already had his anesthesia resident's ear when Gianni came in.

"Anthony, we meet again."

"Hello, Larry. Sorry to have to be the one to drag you in here tonight."

"No big deal, if it wasn't you it would have been someone with some bogus emergency. Like the patient who's been lying around the hospital for three days and suddenly becomes an emergency when the surgeon is done with his office schedule. You know how it goes. But I saw your guy and he clearly needs some attention."

They reassembled in the OR suite. Rosen was talking non-stop to the resident. He was an effective teacher, actually. On the OR table, the patient had already been anesthetized and an endotracheal tube placed through his nose. The injury had filleted his face open from a point above the right ear and extending down below the jaw. The internal part of the wound looked like a piece of raw steak, bright red against the dark complexion of the patient's skin.

Gianni then began to quiz his own understudy. "Okay Matt, what's the pertinent anatomy here, what are we worried about?"

"Well, I checked the facial nerve and it looks like all of the five branches on the face are grossly intact."

"After we're scrubbed you can recite for me the course of the facial nerve from its origin on out to the terminal branches, including all of the branches."

"You mean the five on the face?"

"I mean those five plus the six before those. Why don't you think about that."

"Um, okay."

"And what else are we concerned about here, Dr. Kantor?"

"The parotid duct."

"Do you think it got cut?"

"I'm not sure. I thought we'd look under better lighting in the OR."

"All right," Gianni said. "Go ahead and scrub, he's intubated already and I want to get a photograph or two for the record." He snapped three photographs of the wound, then joined Kantor in the scrub room. In the OR, they prepared and draped the patient for the procedure. Kantor asked for some music.

"Is it okay if I play one of mine, Dr. Gianni?"

"It'll probably keep me awake, at least."

"Can we put in that Bon Jovi tape?" Kantor asked the circulating nurse.

"Believe it or not, I have a Bon Jovi album myself," Gianni said.

The music began to play:

Why you wanna to tell me how to run my life!

"Great song," Kantor said.

"Figures," Gianni said.

Who are you to tell me if it's black or white!

"So where do you want to start, Matt?"

"With the jaw fracture, inside to out. Right?"

"That's fine. We should be able to get enough exposure to place a small plate right through the wound."

He began a careful blunt dissection, cut through the masseter muscle and aligned the bone fragments. Gianni adapted and secured a small bone plate to fix the broken fragments together.

"Now how about that parotid duct, Matt?"

"Shit, I forgot my loupes," Matt said. "You have yours on. Can you find it?"

"I already have found it. But I thought, since you've never seen one of these, you might have at least had the foresight to bring your own goddamn loupes. And where the hell were you when the ER was paging you?"

Kantor looked up nervously for a moment, then watched as Gianni located the two cut ends of the parotid duct, the structure that carried saliva from the salivary gland into the mouth. If left unrepaired, saliva would either pool in the wound and create an infection, or else drain out through a fistula in the face, rather than flowing into the mouth.

"Lacrimal probes and the twenty gauge catheter please," Gianni said. He was ready to join the two ends over a small hollow catheter that would act as a scaffold to keep the duct open until the initial healing took place. It would also serve to keep the duct from scarring down and closing itself off to the proper flow of saliva.

"So where were you?" he asked Kantor again.

"Having dinner with my fiancé. It was a nice restaurant so I didn't want my cell phone on."

"Your phone doesn't have a silent mode? Or your pager? Jesus Christ, Matt, are you for real? While you were munching your damn *foie gras*, I was preparing the patient for the OR. What the hell is wrong with that picture!"

Kantor said nothing.

"When I was a second year resident," Gianni said, "we were required to be physically present in the ER until eleven every single night that we were on call. We saw a lot of interesting stuff that way and no one particularly complained. Enough of that. What kind of suture to repair the duct, Matt?"

"6-0 Vicryl?"

"No, finer even. Of course, without your loupes, you'd be hard pressed to see it. I'll finish that part and then let you start a nice layered repair."

He had Kantor begin to repair the wound in layers, which he did with a certain proficiency despite a fine tremor evident in both hands.

"That's looking good, Matt," Gianni said, sensing his resident's need for reassurance.

"You know, Dr. Gianni, I think my generation just has different priorities. It's all about quality of life."

"And how about responsibility?"

"I don't know, Dr. Gianni. Have you ever read *The Fountainhead*?"

"I have, and this is not a literature class," Gianni said. "So let's not get distracted here. We can work together on the skin closure. Brenda, can you re-start that tape again. That wasn't half bad."

They spent the last half hour on a very exacting closure of skin, to the music of Bon Jovi.

This is the story of my life

And I write it every day

I know it isn't black and white

And it's anything but grey

I know that no, I'm not all right

But I'll be O.K. because

Anything can, everything can happen

That's the story of my life

GIANNI INSPECTED THE FINAL repair. The man now had an intact face that appeared ruggedly handsome.

"Matt, why don't you dictate the operative report," Gianni said, handing him a sticker with the patient's name on it. He took a second sticker for himself and placed it in his scrub shirt pocket.

He then took the familiar walk through the corridors to his office in the Doctors' Pavilion. He sat at his desk and glanced at the pile of mail. He opened only one letter, a memo from Bushmill Stable.

> *TO: All partners in Chiefly Endeavor*
>
> *We believe that Chiefly Endeavor is a three-year-old with great potential. His pedigree would suggest that he can run on dirt as well as grass. We have entered him in the Grade I Florida Derby at Gulfstream on March 30th. This is a mile-and-an-eighth on the dirt. While this will be a relatively long layoff from his last race, he seems to require a longer rest period than most. He is a talented colt and we should use him sparingly. I trust you will agree.*
>
> *Stuart G. Duncker*
>
> *President, Bushmill Stable*

Gianni set the letter aside and smiled. The Florida Derby was one of the major prep races for the Kentucky Derby. He then took the sticker from the operating room out of his pocket and set it onto another area of his desk. He read the name aloud, last name first: *Giardini, Hector.*

Chapter 9

The woman walked across the room and looked at the envelope on the dresser. Thumbing it casually, she noted that it contained a wad of hundred dollar bills. She did not count them.

She appeared to be in her early thirties with a trim and athletic body, blonde hair and a stunningly beautiful face. Deep blue eyes looked directly into his. Her small nose was perfectly sculpted, without any surgery, it seemed. She brushed back a fallen tassel of hair and smiled, declining Gianni's offer of a drink from the minibar.

The room at the Delano Hotel was all white. White walls, bedcovers, and white sheer drapes floated in the breeze from the open glass doors. A peach colored bouquet of flowers sat on a glass table, providing the only color apart from the ocean and the clear blue sky. The ocean air was warm and it was nearing sunset.

She walked towards Gianni and embraced him, her arms around him, her hands finding his neck. The scent of her perfume was delicate yet alluring. Lilacs, he thought. She kissed him deeply and lingered a long time before dropping to her knees. Clothes were flung to the floor.

"This is my favorite," she said. She lingered there as well, then took his hand in hers and led him to the bed. Almost imperceptibly, she rolled on a condom and straddled his body, teasing him with gentle kisses. She seemed to enjoy it when he was finally inside her, if her chants were any indication. They were subtle, intense, genuine he thought.

"Sex is *so amazing*," she said.

Gianni jumped up, breathing heavily when the alarm went off. He looked around the room and tried to recollect where he was. His breathing slowed. As the sleep faded, he gradually oriented himself. *Florida…the Delano Hotel…Florida Derby Day…Chiefly Endeavor.* He hadn't set the alarm in his hotel room and was startled from a sound sleep when it went off. *But the dream was so real. Why did he have it? Nothing he would ever do, he thought.*

He would often try to recall or analyze his dreams, and could usually link the content to an event from the past day. He remembered that the governor of New York had once been linked to a prostitution ring and was forced to resign in disgrace. It had come up in a recent conversation. Perhaps that explained the content, but the intensity? Freud said dreams were often about wish fulfillment. Would *he* ever be so unrighteous?

Gianni recalled that when he heard the news of the government official, he was incredulous, wondering how a man at the pinnacle of his career could flush it all in a moment of indiscretion. The same official had actually prosecuted prostitution rings during his time as Attorney General. Yet the very powerful come to feel entitled and infallible. They take risks and seek excitement, even though it may be momentary, expensive, and dangerous. Gianni then thought of a quote from a character in a Robert Dugoni novel—something about being God-fearing ninety-five percent of the time and a sinner the other five percent. It was the five percent that got people in trouble, when they succumbed to a weakness or just did something plain stupid.

With that analysis, he dismissed the dream and began to focus on the day ahead. Chiefly Endeavor was set to run in the Florida Derby, one of the major prep races for the Kentucky Derby. He was alone at the hotel. Janice once again had business at home. Brad Hill also remained in New York. Stu Duncker was recovering from hip surgery, so Gianni and Chet would be forced to get better acquainted. Gianni looked forward to that with little enthusiasm, to say the least. He would focus mainly on the horse and perhaps try to learn a little more about his new partner as well.

TEN PALMS RESTAURANT is on level two at Gulfstream Park. A plenteous buffet had been assembled for the owners, trainers and others who had connections with the horses entered in stakes races that day. It included a carving station with slices of rare prime rib and freshly roasted turkey. There were a variety of pasta specialties, tomato and buffalo mozzarella salad, marinated artichokes, all sorts of freshly baked breads, salmon and blackened mahi mahi, and more.

Anthony and Chet were seated at a table for four. A waitress arrived to take their drink order.

"What kind of beer do you have?" Chet asked.

The waitress said, "Too many to remember. What kind do you want?"

"Do you have Guinness?"

"On tap," she said.

"Pint of Guinness and a cognac, Courvoisier," Chet said.

"And for you, sir?"

"Can I get an iced coffee, please?" Gianni asked.

Chet looked at him quizzically. "You a teetotaler?"

"No, I just don't like drinking during the day. It makes me feel too logy. I like a clear head for a big race day."

When the drinks arrived, Chet raised a brandy sniffer and said, "Well, here's to Chiefly Endeavor." He slugged it down in a single swallow, and then followed it with several gulps of beer.

"Shall we eat," Chet announced as he stood up to head towards the buffet tables.

He returned with two plates, a large dinner plate heaped into several large piles that included virtually everything that had been offered. The piles mixed together so that they blended into some sort of monumental goulash. At the bottom of the heap were double portions of the beef and turkey. On the smaller plate were several types of salad, a little more distinct from one another than the giant goulash on the larger plate.

"What a spread, huh?"

Gianni looked across at the two plates. "Looks more like a heap than a spread there on your plate, Chet."

"All goes to the same place, Doc." He patted his belly, which protruded noticeably from his unbuttoned sport coat. The top two buttons of his shirt were open and a heavy gold chain was visible amidst the forest of black and grey hair. The chain disappeared into the shirt, and Gianni wondered what hung at the end of it—a medallion, crucifix, maybe nothing.

Chet looked across at Gianni's plate. "What's wrong with you? You on a diet?"

Gianni had selected roast turkey, a pasta salad, and the tomato with buffalo mozzarella. "No, I'm just not in the mood for a big meal. I'll have my dinner celebration tonight."

Regardless of the amount of food Gianni had on his plate, he would invariably finish it quickly, but without any appearance of eating too fast. It was more a deliberate pace, not a rushed one, something that he had acquired during his residency training. He remembered that at the time, his colleagues would often skip a lunch rather than try to wolf something down in five or ten minutes. He would always sit and eat, even if for only a few minutes. If he didn't, he wouldn't function well for the remainder of the day. He thought then, and he thought now, how terrible it must feel to go hungry for days, or longer, as some of the world's impoverished must do. Then he thought of his upcoming medical mission to the island of St. Lucia. He had spent much of the previous week assembling the required credentialing files and completing the application.

Across the table, Chet looked like a human shovel, devouring large forkfuls of mixed portions in a shark-like feeding frenzy. Gianni imagined that if there had been another fork at his side, he might be using one in each hand. He did need the free hand though, because the fistfuls of food were punctuated by gulps of beer. When the glass was empty, he turned his head side to side looking for the waitress. When he spotted her, he raised his empty glass in her direction and she soon returned with another Guinness.

Few words were spoken for the next several minutes. Knowing

he was a fast eater, Gianni was amazed when Chet finished just shortly after him, though Chet's speed and voracity were clearly evident.

When Chet returned from the desert table, Gianni noted that he had been a little more selective for his final feeding, choosing only a piece of key lime pie and a slice of dark chocolate cake.

"Where will you watch the race?" Gianni inquired.

"We have a box, don't we?" Chet asked.

"So does Jeff, in a different area, though. Jeff can get a little superstitious about certain things, so if he does well with his horse in the sixth race, I'd be willing to bet that he'll want to stay in the same spot for our race. So I may join him there, or wherever he's headed."

Chet had not quite finished desert when he began to tell Gianni a story about the superstitions of a certain well-known trainer. As he spoke, a mixture of key lime and chocolate moved about in his open mouth.

"They say this guy is so superstitious that he can never stop the gas pump with any combination of the number thirteen on the meter, you know, like thirteen dollars, thirteen g-g-gallons. So if he tops off his tank at thirteen something, he keeps pumping the gas, right on the pavement, until it hits fourteen."

"You know the story of the Kentucky Derby Trophy?" Gianni asked.

"What about it?"

"They changed the trophy in 1999 for the 125th running so that the horseshoe on the gold cup has the open end pointed up instead of down. It was done because superstition decrees that if the horseshoe is turned down, all the luck will run out."

"Really? No shit?"

Gianni felt for the knot in his necktie, straightened it, then fastened the top button of his navy blue, cotton suit coat. "I have some people I need to see. I'll see you in the paddock before the race. Let me take care of the bar tab and leave something for our waitress. The buffet is on the house, I guess you know, so it's just the drinks and her tip."

Gianni fully expected to pay but was surprised that Chet didn't even raise a token objection or offer to contribute. Instead, Chet summoned the waitress one last time. "How about a coffee, dear?"

Gianni looked at Chet and thought, *My new partner— a slob and a skinflint, too.*

GIANNI WAS HAPPY to leave Chet behind and find Jeff Willard in the paddock area before the race. Jeff seemed more nervous than usual, and even Chiefly Endeavor seemed a little more high-strung, his dark bay coat beginning to lather in the sun. Rafael Bejarano would ride Chiefly Endeavor again this time, and Jeff put his arm around the jockey and said, "Leave him covered up, behind some horses, but not too far back. If he's running mid pack on the backstretch, I'll be happy. You'll know when to make the move."

By the time Chet waddled into the paddock, the jockeys had already taken their mounts and the horses were parading around the cramped Gulfstream paddock. Chiefly Endeavor pranced in line with the others, then exited the paddock and prepared to join his lead pony out on the main track.

As Chiefly Endeavor left the paddock, a fan shouted loudly, "Go Rafael, you're the man." Bejarano smiled at the fan and raised two fingers in a "V" sign.

Gianni and Chet followed their trainer to a box just off the finish line, near the sixteenth pole. As Chiefly Endeavor walked by for the post parade, his rear legs gave a sideways cow-kick in the direction of his pony, causing the pony and rider to trot away.

"He's never done that before," Gianni said. "What the hell is wrong, Jeff?"

Jeff said nothing and remained focused on the post parade of horses, alternating his gaze from binoculars to the track. Chiefly Endeavor seemed to settle once his lead pony trotted away. Five minutes later, the relatively small field of seven horses lined up in the gate, and the announcer began his call of the race.

THEY'RE ALL IN LINE. AND THEY'RE OFF AND RUNNING IN THE FLORIDA DERBY. BROTHER BIRD BREAKS WELL, FOLLOWED CLOSELY BY ATONED...OH, NO— CHIEFLY ENDEAVOR HAS STUMBLED AT THE GATE, HE STUMBLED BADLY AND IS NOW WELL BACK BEHIND THE OTHER HORSES.

"Damn it! Is he all right?" Gianni said. He stood up and continued to follow the horse's every stride through his binoculars.

SO IT'S BROTHER BIRD, CONTINUING TO SET THE PACE WITH ATONED JUST TO HIS OUTSIDE. THEN A GAP OF TWO TO REVENGENCE AND SACRED DANCE, WITH RIVERADO SAVING GROUND ON THE RAIL. AND THE QUARTER WENT IN 23 AND 3. ONLY EIGHT LENGTHS SEPARATES THE FIRST AND LAST HORSES NOW, AS CHIEFLY ENDEAVOR HAS RECOVERED NICELY AND STARTED TO RALLY AT THE BACK OF THE PACK.

"He's moving well, now," Jeff said.

"Goddamn," Chet hollered. "Goddamn."

THE HALF WENT IN 46 AND 3. SO THE PACE REMAINS STRONG, AND THEY'LL ALL HAVE TO CATCH BROTHER BIRD, WHO HAS OPENED A FIVE LENGTH LEAD AS THEY ROUND THE FAR TURN.

The announcer then screamed a guttural…

AND DOWN THE STRETCH THEY COME! BROTHER BIRD
CONTINUES TO LEAD. JUST BEHIND HIM ARE SACRED DANCE
AND REVENGENCE, THOSE TWO NECK AND NECK, HEADS
BOBBING AS THEY NEAR THE EIGHTH POLE. AND NOW
CONTINUING TO RALLY FROM THE BACK OF THE PACK, HERE
COMES CHIEFLY ENDEAVOR, PASSING HORSES AND SUDDENLY
FLYING TOWARD THE WIRE. CHIEFLY ENDEAVOR HAS JUST
MADE A REMARKABLE, A SPECTACULAR LAST TO FIRST RUN,
RECOVERING FROM A STUMBLE AT THE GATE TO WIN THE
FLORIDA DERBY… AND THE TIME IS 1:47.82, A NEW TRACK
RECORD ON THIS VERY FAST TRACK HERE AT GULFSTREAM
PARK. BROTHER BIRD HELD ON FOR SECOND AND REVENGENCE
WAS THIRD.

In the winner's circle, a horseshoe shaped blanket of lavender orchids, seven feet long, was draped over horse and jockey. Gianni and Jeff Willard congratulated Rafael on his masterful ride, and Gianni patted the horse's neck, wiping away some of the foamy lather.

While it was certainly a proud moment, Gianni cringed when Chet, more full of himself than ever, rumbled, "On to the Kentucky Derby."

Chapter 10

The 88 year old man was wheeled into Dr. Gianni's office and ushered to a treatment room. Matt Kantor, the senior resident, was observing Gianni in his office for the day, and he had ordered the elderly man transferred from the emergency department.

The man had extensive bruising extending from his forehead to his neck, and the sclera of his right eye was bright red with blood. He had a stubbly white beard and thinning white hair, partially caked with dried blood. His chest and shoulders were slumped forward in the wheelchair, and a wide Velcro strap kept him partially secured in the chair.

Kantor was eager to take over in his evaluation of the new patient, and Gianni let him do so. Standing beside the man's wheelchair, Kantor asked, "So what happened, Mr. Farrell?"

"Fell out of a chair," the man said.

"And I see you are on Aricept, Diovan, Colace and aspirin? Anything else?"

"Whatever they give me."

"Whatever who gives you?" Kantor asked.

"You know, the folks at the home."

Kantor began to palpate the man's cheek bone, while Gianni looked at a CT scan of the facial bones on a laptop computer that sat atop an adjustable stand in the corner of the examining room.

"How are his eye movements?" Gianni asked.

"No sign of entrapment, he's following my finger just fine."

"Any impingement of the coronoid?" Gianni asked.

"No, the jaw moves well, good excursions."

"So what do you think then, Matt?" Gianni asked.

Kantor spoke to the patient. "Mr. Farrell, have they told you that your cheek bone is fractured?"

"Nope, nobody told me that."

"Well it is, on the right side. We could do an operation to fix it."

Gianni looked up from the screen, surprised to hear Kantor discuss surgery for the frail, elderly gentleman.

"It would be mainly for esthetics, though," Kantor said.

Farrell looked up at Kantor, gave a sideways glance over at Gianni and said, "It's a little late for that."

Gianni laughed and said, "I think Mr. Farrell has just given a very informed refusal for this operation." He went over to Farrell, crouching to a stoop and meeting the old man's gaze at eye level and said, "We can check you again in a week or two, just to make sure everything is okay."

"Thanks, Doc."

"Do you have any family with you that you'd like us to speak with?" Gianni asked.

"No, just me. Wife died two years ago."

"I'm sorry. Any sons or daughters?"

"I have a son in California, but...I don't get to see him much. They say I'm still competent to make my own decisions, you know."

"I'm sure you are," Gianni said. "We'll see you next week, okay?"

"Sure, next week."

Gianni turned to his resident and said, "Let's go into my private office, Matt. We can review this CT together."

While Gianni waited for Matt to discharge the patient and join him in the office, he took a waiting call from Stu Duncker. "Morning, Stu."

"Anthony, I'm calling about Chiefly Endeavor. You know that he came out of that race quite sore, and there's a little heat in that left front shin. We'll do an ultrasound, though the vet doesn't really suspect any structural issues. The bottom line is that he won't be ready for a race in two weeks. We all had our hearts set on the Kentucky Derby, but I'm afraid it's not meant to be. I'm terribly disappointed."

"Naturally, I am too. But I understand, and would never want to chance something that wouldn't be in the horse's best interest. So maybe with a little rest, he'll still make it to the Preakness, right? Maybe it's a blessing in disguise."

"Do you know the Winston Churchill quote about blessing in disguise?" Duncker said.

"I don't."

Duncker said, "Following World War II, when he lost the general election in 1945, his wife said just that. 'Maybe it's a blessing in disguise.' To which Churchill replied, 'If it is, then it's certainly a damn good disguise.'"

Chapter 11

Saratoga Springs, NY
Two months later

Gianni and Jeff Willard sat at one end of the L-shaped bar in Chianti Il Ristorante, beginning a debate about who might be the greatest race track announcer of all time. It was exactly two days after the running of the Preakness Stakes.

"So who was it?" Jeff said. "Who was the greatest track announcer of all time?

Gianni looked up at a rack of assorted glasses above their heads, extending nearly the entire length of the bar. A row of small light fixtures was suspended from the ceiling, sending flickers of soft light through the glasses. "You mean in my lifetime?" he said.

"In your lifetime," Jeff said.

"My God, there have been so many. I always remember Fred Caposella as a kid, then Chic Anderson and Marshall Cassidy. Tom Durkin is fantastic— I love his calls, very theatrical. I miss Vic Stauffer at Gulfstream. Remember his call at one of the California tracks when an earthquake erupted right during the race. Collmus is good too, but…"

"Okay, okay," Jeff interrupted. "Let me rephrase the question: What was the best race call of all time for you personally?"

Gianni smiled. "No question about that one. The best race call of all time for me personally was when Dave Johnson bellowed: '...AND DOWN THE STRETCH THEY COME IN THE PREAKNESS AND CHIEFLY ENDEAVOR IS DRAWING CLEAR.'"

Jeff grinned and raised his glass high. "To the best race call of all time. Chiefly Endeavor's win in the Preakness Stakes, last Saturday, Pimlico Race Course."

Their wine glasses clinked.

"So now what?" Gianni asked.

"Well, he's been somewhat plagued by sore shins ever since he came off the turf and switched to dirt. It's an evolutionary flaw, really, that's left the thoroughbred with these delicate, trifurcated suspensory ligaments that sit in spindly legs, with a ton of solid muscle working above."

"Can he go back to the turf?" Gianni asked.

"I don't know, Doc. He'll be coming up here this week. Let's just hope his ultrasound doesn't show any holes or tears in the ligaments. We'll give him some time off, and as long as the ultrasound is clear, we'll let him gallop on the main track, or maybe even use the half mile oval in Claire Court. It's soft, and usually kind on the horses, good for a gentle gallop. I certainly wouldn't rule out a move to turf either."

"Duncker mentioned that he'd like to think about running in the Travers Stakes," Gianni said. "If he can stay sound running on dirt that would be fantastic, but there are certainly plenty of good opportunities on turf too."

"The Travers is certainly a possibility, and we have a good three months to decide. Then too, even if he never races again, he's a son of Dynaformer and a Classic winner, so he has tremendous potential as a sire. After Barbaro, and with Dynaformer getting on in years, Kentucky would love to see Chiefly Endeavor in the breeding shed."

"No doubt, that day will come," Gianni said, "but I sure would like to see him campaign as a four-year-old. Right now, I'm starving. Shall we get a table?"

Chapter 12

Five days later, Gianni's spirits were still soaring from the Preakness win when he passed through the security gate on Union Avenue in Saratoga, entering the backstretch area of the Oklahoma training track. He drove towards the rail of the track and parked on the grass facing the stretch run.

A huge Hummer H2 drove up to the rail a few car lengths away, and Gianni noted the vanity plate…THE LUZ. *Who the hell would that be?* Gianni wondered. The door opened and out dropped Mike Luzzi, complete with helmet and flak jacket. Anyone would have looked small standing next to the mammoth SUV, but the compact jockey seemed particularly eclipsed by the vehicle. He was greeted by a chorus of "Hey Luz" from several of the dozen or so who stood along the rail watching the horses.

Well I'll be damned, I never knew he was "The Luz," Gianni thought, though he certainly knew of his ability and popularity as a rider. His thoughts were interrupted by the shrill of a siren, a warning usually indicating a loose horse that had either unseated a rider or become otherwise unmanageable. A frisky looking two-year-old was on the loose, bucking and galloping in the wrong direction, weaving around the few horses whose riders had not yet brought them to a secure stopping point along the outer rail.

Gianni raised his binoculars and looked across the track. He recognized the unseated rider as Manuel, one of Jeff Willard's most experienced exercise riders. Manuel walked with a slight limp, but appeared mostly unscathed by the fall. A year earlier, an equally experienced rider from another barn hadn't been so lucky, sustaining a fatal head injury after a fall on the same track.

Gianni then recognized Jeff Willard, galloping by on Amigo, his stable pony. Trainers sometimes watched their horses from the viewing stand, or sometimes joined the exercise riders on horseback themselves, to take advantage of that unique vantage point and the greater mobility. Jeff galloped up behind the loose two-year-old, and with the aplomb of a rodeo star, he rode alongside the horse, grabbed the loose rein and slowed both horses to a trot, then to a walk. The crowd that had gathered along the rail let out a cheer.

One of them yelled, "Hey Willard, if you weren't so damn big, you'd make a hell of a jockey."

"Easier than roping a calf," Jeff yelled back.

A second siren signaled the all clear, and Jeff passed the reins off to another one of his riders, who walked the colt slowly off the track and back to his barn. Manuel walked along the grass outside the perimeter of the rail. He seemed fine now, with only his pride possibly hurting a bit.

Jeff stopped Amigo alongside the rail, close to where Gianni was standing.

"Nice work," Gianni said. "Is Chiefly Endeavor slated for a work today?"

Jeff appeared flustered. "You mean you don't know?" he said.

"Don't know what?"

Jeff grimaced and said, "I'll be damned, you really don't know."

"Jeff, what the hell is it?" Gianni said.

"Chiefly Endeavor shipped back to Kentucky on Wednesday."

"Jesus Christ, when was someone going to tell *me* that?"

"I'm sorry, Doc, but you know Duncker likes to deliver all the bad news himself. I had no idea that you weren't in the loop."

"So what's the problem?" Gianni asked.

"We did another ultrasound here and it seemed to show an actual tear in the suspensory ligament, the front left. So naturally, Stu wanted him to go right to Rood and Riddle to get their expert opinion."

Duncker always favored the very well regarded equine clinic in Lexington for any potentially serious malady.

"Well, I'm all for that, I just would have liked it if someone had let me know what the hell was up."

Gianni walked away from the rail, opened the door to his jeep, threw his binoculars onto the seat and grabbed his cell phone, speed dialing Stu Duncker.

"Stu, it's Anthony."

"Anthony, I was just about to call you."

"Just about to call? After three days? I have to find out my horse is in Kentucky after a two hour drive from Westchester to Saratoga?"

"Wait a minute," Duncker said. Didn't you get a call from my office on Wednesday? I asked Sandy to let you know that we wanted to have the horse evaluated by Dr. Copelan."

"I knew nothing until I arrived here this morning."

"I am truly sorry. It's been a little crazy around here so I asked Sandy to help me with some of the calls. Today, I was planning to call you myself because I just got the results of Dr. Copelan's evaluation last night, and I'm afraid it's not good."

Gianni was silent.

Duncker continued, "There is a significant tear in the suspensory ligament. Dr. Copelan doesn't think it is necessarily career ending, but it would require an extended period of rehabilitation, at least six months. That would put us into December, and there would be no guarantee that he would be as sharp as he had been. In my experience with these types of injuries, and with this severity, horses never return to the same level of fitness."

"And…he could always injure himself again," Gianni said quietly.

"That's absolutely right. On the other hand, he is perfectly able to function as a stallion, and we have already had some very attractive offers from some of the leading breeders in Kentucky. If we retire him now, he could begin stallion duty this next season. One year later, we'll see his first foals. I think it's the best thing for the horse, Anthony."

"Have you talked to Chet?" Gianni asked.

"Not yet, but Chet has been anxious to retire him for stud duty even before this injury. It seems to be more about the dollars and cents where Chet is concerned."

There was another long silence.

"I suppose it is best if we retire him," Gianni said. "I expect that

Brad Hill will follow my lead, which will make it unanimous. Though if Chet wants him retired, then we already have a majority, so I guess that's a moot point."

"It's the right decision, Anthony. I'm confident of that."

Chapter 13

Saratoga Springs, NY

The auction ring at the Fasig Tipton Pavilion is reminiscent of a two-tiered theater in the round, and its most celebrated show is the Saratoga Selected Yearlings Sale in August. The stage is a round ring of green sawdust, set off by a sturdy, ornate rope and sculptured horse heads. Horses enter and leave the ring from two separate doors behind the auction ring.

At a podium stood two men in tuxedos. One announced the horse as it entered the ring. He spoke with a distinguished British accent. "Number 164 from Eaton Sales is a grey or roan colt, by Unbridled's Song, out of Home Court. Loads of class here, by the grade one winner of 1.3 million, sire of sixty-five stakes winners. The dam is stakes placed, and is a full sister to stakes winner One Nice Cat. This is her second foal, her first is a current two-year-old. This colt has the size, he has the looks, and he moves beautifully."

The auctioneer then began, in speech so rapid the uninitiated would consider it gibberish. "One hundred thousand, do I hear two now two. One fifty then, will you give one fifty, and now two, two, who will give two now, two. Two hundred thousand upstairs, now do I have two fifty now, two twenty-five then."

Four spotters, also clad in formal wear, stood strategically around the ring. They knew who the likely bidders were, and they spotted the slightest nod, or a scarcely raised finger. It all happened with lightning speed.

"Now three. Do I hear three hundred thousand? Three, three…"

The bidding had slowed, and while the auctioneer paused, the announcer spoke into the microphone to entice the bidders. "He's too good looking for this price folks. He's got his sire written all over him and he has a great walk. Take another look at him."

The auctioneer resumed, "Now three. Do we have 350? Do I hear 375? Will you give 375? And now four, do I hear four? Now four. Who will give 450? Now 450. Do I hear 450? Do I hear 475? Now 475. Do I hear 500 thousand? 475, 500. Five hundred. Five hundred."

The spotters flashed hand signals, raised and jiggled four or five fingers and shouted as the bids continued. "Hup…Here." They would all make great pit traders on the Commodities Exchange, Gianni thought as he followed the action. Chester Pawlek sat next to him in the upstairs gallery. An empty chair separated the two men.

The auctioneer slowed his voice for the first time since the bidding had begun, wanting to be sure to allow any final bids. "Five, 520…five, 520…520, yes or no, 520."

The horse in the ring whinnied, as if to proclaim his worth. Gianni leaned over and whispered to Chet, "Don't scratch your nose now, or you may be out 500 K."

"How do you know I don't want him?" Chet asked.

The gavel came down with a loud clap. "Sold, five hundred thousand, upstairs."

"That wasn't you, was it?" Gianni asked.

"Reynolds, I think."

"Let's take a break," Gianni said.

As they walked the perimeter of the upstairs gallery, Gianni paused to look at some of the artwork. Many of the oil paintings, most of them equine themed, would sell for as much as some of the yearlings.

Chet apparently couldn't resist boasting. "I bought one of the big ones for my trophy room last year," he said.

"Construction business must be pretty good," Gianni said.

"What?"

"The oil painting," Gianni said. "They're certainly not cheap."

"Oh, yeah. We…got some nice bids," Chet said.

"Where?" Gianni asked.

"You know, down on the Island."

As they walked down the stairs, a pretty young lady ran past them, disrupting their conversation as she headed up the stairs with the ticket for the high bidder to sign. Outside the pavilion, horses continued to be escorted from their barns to the walking area outside the two doors that opened into the auction ring. Gianni and Chet strolled past the walking area and headed towards the bar. Behind a large, polished mahogany bar, the walls were decorated with photographs of some of racing's great historical figures.

"Grey Goose on the rocks, please," Gianni said.

"Whoa, holy shit, the doctor's drinking. I guess I'm buying. This is a first."

"What, you buying?" Gianni chided.

"No, you drinking," Chet said. "Brandy and a beer for me." The bartender seemed to know Chet, and brought him Courvoisier and Guinness.

"I told you, I'm not a teetotaler, just certain times, not all the time," Gianni said.

"And I'm more than happy to let you buy tonight. After all, you just closed one hell of a deal on the Chiefly Endeavor syndicate."

From his coat pocket, Chet produced a large cigar, a Churchill. Even in his pudgy hand, it looked huge. "Yeah, g-g-guess I did. I figure, why not keep my fifty-percent stake. Those stud fees will just keep on coming." Chet downed the Courvoisier and thumped the oversized shot glass on the bar. "I'll take another brandy here," he said to the bartender. He lit the cigar with a gold butane lighter, first heating the end with the flame, then twirling the cigar and drawing hard through tightly pursed lips. The flame grew several inches high around the end of the cigar. When the end was red with hot ash, he shut down the lighter and exhaled a cloud of smoke in Gianni's direction.

Gianni said, "I thought about keeping more of my stake than I did. But I'm really more interested in the racing end of things. I like the excitement of racing, and the peace and quiet of the mornings at the training track. I'm happy with my breeding rights for two seasons."

"We had a good run with him, huh?" Chet said, drinking the second brandy at a slightly slower pace. His large, bulbous nose seemed to grow redder with each swallow.

Gianni said, "That we did. Stakes winner on grass and dirt. The Florida Derby and the Preakness, for God's sake. Too bad we had to retire him as early as we did. I'd have loved to see him race another year."

"I'm happy just the way things are," Chet said, taking another generous drag on his cigar and holding the smoke in his mouth.

"I know you are, but the sport needs more horses that race longer. It needs to bring in more fans, and that requires star horses with some soundness, horses that can race for a few good years."

"Maybe so. But it's hard to pass up that big price for a move to the breeding shed," Chet said, turning his head away from Gianni and releasing the smoke from his mouth.

"Well, in the Chief's case there was no good alternative. I love that damn horse, Chet, and I've always wanted to do what was best for him. I don't think his suspensory ligaments would have held up. Still, I'll miss seeing him on the track. I'll miss my early morning visits. And I wish to God he could be running in the Travers this month, like we originally planned. I saw him just yesterday morning and he looks fantastic. Mean as hell, but fantastic."

"Did he try to bite you again, Anthony? You really ought to be careful, you might l-l-lose a goddamn finger or something."

"No, he's all right. You just can't turn your back on him."

"I know a lot of p-p-people like that," Chet said.

Gianni watched his boorish companion down the rest of the brandy and the beer and thought, *I imagine you do.*

Chapter 14

Newark, NJ

When a man is hunted, simple freedoms are lost until the hunt has ended and a victor declared. With many in the mob, the hunt becomes a way of life, and to function as good gangsters, they become oblivious to the constant threats to self and to family.

But Chester Pawlek had always been different. As a Polish American, he considered himself an outsider. He was drawn into the mob life in his later years, and he never got over the loss of freedom and the perpetual fear. He would hesitate momentarily when he started his car. Would this be the morning it exploded and burned? He worried walking into a restaurant, always seeking a table near the corner where he could have his back to a wall. He never liked to have his back to any open doorway, and he had developed the nervous habit of constantly looking over his shoulder, even as he spoke to a friend or a business associate in an office building.

Chet often recalled with great nostalgia the train rides from New York to Florida in his youth—the sense of relaxation and freedom, watching the scenery change, counting the station stops and the states traversed. Now he imagined he would never again set foot on a passenger train, fearing he might be followed into a sleeper car and terminated, right there, in the berth of his once cozy retreat. He could still count the station stops, but now in every station he would be forced to view the new passengers, and regard each one as an imminent foe.

He thought of those earlier train rides as he drove under the freight tracks in a remote area of Newark. He had driven there alone, just as he had been instructed, and he circled once past the parked black sedan before returning again and stopping face-to-face with the vehicle. He turned the headlights off and tried to see into the other car. There was no way to penetrate the tinted glass of the Lincoln, but he had been told there would be only two men. Chet carried no weapon, and he got out of the vehicle and lifted his empty hands just high enough to indicate their innocence, never wanting to raise them in surrender. The two front doors of the Lincoln opened and two men in dark topcoats emerged.

"Chet, good to see you."

Chet recognized the driver as Sal, one of the famed Catroni brothers. The other man stood silent and motionless, arms crossed with a revolver in one hand.

"You know why we're all here, no doubt."

"Sure, Sal," Chet said.

Sal Catroni took a deep drag on his half-smoked cigarette and flicked the butt to the ground near Chet's feet. "The figure is now five million and growing, and time is running short."

"I know Sal, I j-j-just..."

"Just shut your fucking mouth, Chet, and listen. How much do you think that new young stallion of yours is worth, the one you just sent to Kentucky, Chief something or other? I heard you turned down an offer close to ten mill."

"His name is Chiefly Endeavor, and it wasn't quite that much."

"Must have him insured for close to that, no?"

"Not for ten."

"If you want to keep those fucking pastures on your farm nice and green, Chet, then I think I may see an accident about to happen."

Chet didn't respond. The sound of a passing freight train rumbled in the distance.

"Well, there's your repayment plan and then some, Chet, old boy."

"Look, I'd be a fool to even c-c-consider such a thing, even if I could get away with it, which I c-c-couldn't. That horse has the potential to produce twenty times that in his lifetime. There was this famous stallion in the 90s, Alydar, who died under mysterious circumstances and they still whisper about it in some circles."

"So are you saying you need *my* goddamn help with the job, Chet?"

"I'm saying I would never…could never do that. I told you, that young stallion has so much p-p-potential. Give me three years and I'll triple what I owe you from his income alone."

The statue with the gun burst out laughing, his first utterance, and he asked, "How's his book of business look this year, Chet?"

"Well, it's a little light, but we may have priced him a little high.

We might drop his stud fee you know…" Chet looked up at Catroni and the other goon, but before he could finish his plea Catroni raised his voice.

"Listen Chet, we don't want to hear about your fucking limp-dick pony's potential. We don't want to hear about return in three years. You want a goddamn three year term, you go to your fucking bank. Which, by the way I know you can't, because you're already so friggin leveraged they won't loan you shit. So here's the deal. You want to keep mowing those nice green fields on your gentleman farm, with your family there, nice and healthy and all, then we've just outlined your plan for you. And we're prepared to help, farmer man, if we find out that you need it. Thirty days! I'll be watching the news, ready to cry my fucking eyes out when I read about your four-legged hero."

Chapter 15

Chet returned home from his meeting by the train tracks, lachrymose and regretful. Before exiting his car, he looked into the rear view mirror to be sure his eyes were dry before he went into the house. Chet regretted many things, but mostly he lamented the loss of an earlier time, a time more youthful and more virtuous.

"Hey, John," Chet said when he saw his son on the couch. "Where's your mother?"

"Don't know."

Chet's son John had finally graduated from the New York Military Academy, one term late. In a few weeks he would move to a freshman dorm room at Rutgers University. Since he had been home, there had been a lot of tension between Chet and his wife, resulting in some heated arguments. Chet had ignored the pleas from his wife to keep his voice down, so that it wouldn't echo through the heating grates when he yelled, which he did more often than not. Chet knew that John had a habit of eavesdropping in the hallway down from their bedroom, but it never seemed to curtail his outbursts.

Chet sometimes wondered if his son hated him. He wondered what John might say to his friends about him, as a group of them sat around the large, expansive swimming pool, or hung out in the custom-built recreation room Chet had constructed for his son many years back, in the hope that John and his friends would spend more time at home. Chet had always wanted to monitor their behavior. He feared drugs most of all, for he knew all too well how they could destroy a productive, youthful life.

"Dee! Dee, where are you?"

"Upstairs clean*ing*," Delores shouted back. She spoke with the accent of a New Jersey native.

"What's wrong now, Chet? You look terrible."

"Maybe we should talk." He motioned with a sideways nod and she followed him into the master bedroom. He closed the door behind her.

"You know, Dee, I really shouldn't be discussing business with you."

"Oh God, Chet, Please! Don't make me just another goddamn mafia wife. You know I never talk." As she spoke, she was constantly brushing her hair back with both hands.

"I'd be in some deep shit if you did, Dee."

"Look, Chet, I know there's trouble. For God's sake, you've been hoarding cash like a friggin squirrel. What the hell *is* wrong? And that nervous tic is back. Your eye is twitching right now. Do you realize that?" As she spoke, she looked down at her sweater and began to pick at it, as if retrieving small insects and flicking them onto the floor.

Chet usually kept up a good front. Few knew the extent of his nefarious dealings, only that he seemed to have built a small empire from waste management and land holdings, and parlayed that into a successful thoroughbred racing stable. But in building the horse business, he had leveraged himself to such an extent that he was bleeding cash from the foundation businesses. Any real cash flow he had now stemmed from his illegal activities, and that too was under great pressure as he borrowed from various sources what he was now unable to pay back.

"They met with me again," he confessed to Delores. "They've got this plan, you see. They think if I, you know, make the horse get s-s-sick or something, and God forbid the horse dies, well then we at least have the insurance money."

"Get sick or something? Chet, what are you talking about!"

"I'm just saying, you know, things happen. These horses get sick all the time, or they get injured. Remember when that nice colt we had stepped into a woodchuck hole and boom, the next day he was d-d-dead. And that one wasn't even insured, Dee. Thank God we've got insurance on this one, so if anything were ever to happen…"

"Chet, I don't believe what I'm hearing."

NEITHER DID JOHN PAWLEK, as he listened furtively down the hallway. As John heard his father glossing over the explanation for a crime that had not yet been committed, he couldn't help but wonder if he was actually capable of killing Chiefly Endeavor. He reflected on his father's history and expected he could. That thought sickened him as much as anything he had ever seen or heard about his father.

Chapter 16

Three weeks later

Gianni drove into the parking garage under the Doctor's Pavilion just after six o'clock in the morning. He had the day off—at least he had no scheduled surgery or patient visits. He often arrived early, even on days when his office was closed, to spend time on writing or case planning. He enjoyed the easy morning commute down the Saw Mill Parkway, before the traffic built. Depending on the season, he might see the sun rising off to his left, or the occasional pulse of headlights coming north. He liked the relative quiet of his office and the hospital before the stir of the first shift.

He parked his vehicle and walked to the elevator. As he pushed the elevator button, he saw a leather glove reaching towards his outstretched hand, then felt another gloved hand around his neck. In an instant, a blindfold was placed over his eyes, and the glove covered his mouth.

There appeared to be two men now, one on either side, dragging him away from the elevator, blindfolded, gagged, his arms aching from being twisted behind his back. They pushed him against the side of a car and bound his hands tightly behind his back with duct tape. He heard the car door open, and he was shoved onto a bench seat in the rear of the vehicle. The two front doors then opened and closed, and the vehicle made a series of rapid turns on the ramps, then exited the garage.

The streets were still relatively quiet, and Gianni tried to imagine the route the vehicle was taking. There was no way of knowing, of course, though after several minutes, he thought he recognized the characteristic roar of cars passing side by side in a tunnel. Based on the time that had passed, he figured it was the Lincoln Tunnel and that he was headed to New Jersey.

Apart from the traffic noise and occasional muffled words from the front seat, Gianni heard nothing that gave him any inkling of his abductors' intentions. A kidnapping for ransom, perhaps, but there were far better targets with much deeper pockets than his. He thought about Chet, and wondered if this could have anything to do with him. He fought off surges of nausea and tried to focus on slowing his heart rate. He estimated that about twenty minutes had passed before the vehicle stopped and the engine was turned off. The rear door opened, and a gruff voice said, "Sit up, Doc, we're going to take a little walk." He felt the gloved hands on his arms, pulling him up and out of the door.

"Walk," another voice said, and the two men walked alongside, each of them holding one of Gianni's biceps with a firm grip. When one of the men released his grip, Gianni thought he heard a garage door opening. He was pushed forward a few more steps, then forced onto a chair. The garage door closed, and when the blindfold was removed, he squinted at the light, trying to focus on the two men.

There were no windows, the only light coming from a bare bulb in a ceiling fixture. The walls were all cinder block, except for the metal garage door that had been closed behind them. The room seemed like part of a warehouse, or one of those self-storage units. With the blindfold off, Gianni could see a hint of sunlight where the cinder blocks abutted a tin roof.

Gianni was seated at a metal table with his hands still bound behind his back. At one end of the table stood Sal Catroni. Unlike the other man, he wore no disguise. His longish hair was slicked back neatly, white at the sides, darker on top. His brow was furrowed in a scowl, amplifying the deep frown lines between his black-looking eyes. He held a revolver in front of his chest.

Catroni spoke first. "You know who I am?" he said.

Gianni shook his head.

"I'm Sal Catroni, of the Catroni family, and this here is Hector. Hector was a medic in the marines. He's here to help you with some medical treatment."

Hector stood at least six-two, all of it solid muscle. He wore a tight white dress shirt, its silk sleeves rolled neatly to the middle of his massive forearms. A ski mask, open at the forehead, concealed his face, and his closely cropped black hair stood mostly on end. It reminded Gianni of a 1960s style flat-top cut, only not as stiff.

"Hector has some tools for you, Doc," Catroni said.

Hector opened a clean white linen cloth, the texture of a dishrag but with a starched white appearance. Inside were surgical instruments. Dr. Gianni instantly recognized them—there was a blade handle and several large #10 blades, the kind a surgeon would use to make a long incision. It was not a delicate blade, but one meant to cut hard and fast through a lot of tissue with a single swipe. Next to the blades was a bone cutting forceps, which Gianni knew to be a Rongeurs forceps. Then there was a large pile of neatly folded gauze pads.

"Recognize those tools?" Catroni asked.

Gianni nodded.

"Well, Hector here is prepared to do a little surgery today."

Catroni set his gun aside and cut the tape that bound Gianni's hands, putting his left hand on the table beside the white cloth, and the other hand behind Gianni's back, re-binding it tightly to the chair with duct tape.

"Now Dr. Gianni, Hector here is going to start with the tip of your ring finger, on your left hand. You are right-handed, aren't you?"

"What the hell is this all about?" Gianni said. He tried not to appear flustered. Years of surgical training and interminable hours on call had left him with a coolness under pressure, evident even now.

Catroni continued to talk. "It'll just be the tip, so he won't need that bone cutter, not right off anyway. And of course, we do have a few questions to ask you along the way, and maybe a favor or two, as well."

Hector struggled to put a pair of latex surgical gloves over his huge hands, then attached the blade to the handle with a dexterity that surprised Gianni, given the sheer size of his hands.

Hector said, "Hey, Sal, he's got no ring on it, not even a fucking wedding band. You and Janice still married, Doc? Wouldn't want anything to happen to her either, or would you? Hold still, now, so I only take the tip."

Gianni thought the voice was vaguely familiar.

"You know, when we take a whole finger, we usually take the ring, too. How do you think Sal got that nice two karat diamond he's wearing?" He laughed. "Got it off the finger of this fucking Jew who didn't want to give us the money we had coming. Fucking 'A'!"

He used one hand to reinforce Catroni's grip on Gianni's left hand, isolating the finger and then slicing cleanly through the tip, taking less than an eighth of an inch with the blade cut. The cut was so fast that Gianni barely registered any pain, but he screamed, his sangfroid suddenly gone, when he saw Hector reach for the bone cutter.

"Relax," Hector said, "I just want to clip the nail end, so it's nice and neat. I want it to be nice and neat." He clipped the nail end square and flush with the amputated finger stump. Blood poured out from the cut skin and Gianni winced as Hector grabbed a clump of gauze and squeezed it over the bloody digit.

Catroni then untied Gianni's right hand, and Gianni instinctively clenched the blood drenched gauze in an attempt to slow the bleeding.

"Look," Hector said. "The doctor knows what to do for the bleeding."

Catroni spoke next. "Now you know that will heal just fine in no time. It was only a sliver, after all. And once it does, why, you'll be just as good a surgeon as you ever were, so we have no problem…yet. But the problems will begin when Hector has to do more. Because the next cut is on the next finger over, the middle finger, and just a little farther up. So this time Hector gets to use that bone cutter to clip a little bone, too. Then it's on to the index finger, and a little higher up still. So by the time we get around to the thumb, the whole thing pretty much goes, Doc."

"You stupid bastards. I'll bleed to death, so what the fuck does it matter? Go right ahead. I'm worth more dead than alive if my hands are useless."

"No, no, Dr. Gianni, we wouldn't let that happen. I told you, Hector here is a trained medic."

Hector produced a thick elastic band, a tourniquet, and snapped it against Gianni's arm like a slingshot, mocking him with each slap of the elastic. Gianni knew that the tourniquet could keep him alive. He also knew that left in place long enough, it could also cause him to lose whatever might be left of a mutilated hand, from prolonged lack of blood supply to the vulnerable fingers.

"They taught us in the Marines never to leave these on for too long, but…" Hector shrugged his shoulders, "What the hell, there's a first time to try everything."

"What do you want from me?" Gianni hoped to God it was something other than immediate answers to questions, something that would at least buy him some time. He prayed he might leave this ghastly room today, minus no more than one finger tip.

"You're friends…partners actually, with Chet Pawlek, right?"

"I know him."

"And you own part of that horse Chiefly Endeavor?"

"I kept two breeding rights when Chet bought out the partnership. They're worth about $20,000 each. I'll sign them over to you, that's not a problem."

"Doc, do I look like the kind of guy who would take a few fingers for a lousy 40K?"

Gianni said nothing.

"We want you to make sure your friend Pawlek kills the fucking horse. We've been to him directly, of course, and he's been a little... shall we say, slow to come around."

Gianni's eyes narrowed in anger as he recalled that Chet had asked him some odd medical questions—veterinary questions, really—about certain viral illnesses and unexpected animal deaths.

Catroni continued. "Then we got to thinking, Hector and I did. We figure that big dumb son of a bitch Chester can probably still manage to count all his fucking money with no fingers at all left on his fat hands. But you...well your hands really mean something, I mean they're worth something, aren't they, Doc? So all we're asking is that you show Chet your finger and tell him about our little plan for the rest of your hand...and for his too if necessary. Tell him what a good surgeon Hector here is."

Hector smiled widely, displaying a row of overly white, artificial-looking teeth through the hole in the face mask.

Catroni continued, "You see, we know what kind of man Chet is, which is actually good for you, Doc. Chet never had the stomach for this business—my business that is. He's not the kind of guy who could stand to see his friend the surgeon lose a few fingers. Now me, it wouldn't bother me a bit. For me, it's just business."

Gianni was still holding the bloody bandage around his finger. Briefly removing it, he looked down and it still gushed bright red blood. He reapplied the pressure. The finger throbbed.

Hector came up behind Gianni and blindfolded him again. "Time to go home, Doc. Today's your lucky day...nothing but a little skin off your pinky, right. Don't look no worse for the wear, actually.

Now it's time to show Chet where you had the operation started on your hand. Too bad I couldn't finish it today, huh, Doc?"

Gianni, relieved for the moment, thought back to that first day at the training track with Chiefly Endeavor. He remembered the serenity of the scene, with the fog lifting and the sun becoming more intense. How had he swayed from the serenity of that morning to this wretched, criminal scene.

Chapter 17

Gianni folded his hands on the desk in front of him. The bandage on his ring finger was gone. A small rubber finger cot protected the wound now. Two days had passed since the Catroni incident, and he now contemplated how he would manage the next few days. He dialed the number for Pat Ferris, his long-time office manager.

"Pat," he said, "Sorry to bother you on a Sunday, but I have a little dilemma. Friday after work, I had this freak accident and managed to slice a little sliver off my ring finger."

"Little sliver?" she asked.

"Yeah, a couple millimeters, nothing that could be sutured. But it will have to stay covered for a few more days until I can properly scrub. So I won't be going to the OR for a few days, anyway. I'm at the office looking at my schedule now and…"

"Dr. Gianni, would you care to tell me how this happened, and how serious it is, and never mind your schedule just yet."

"It was this freak accident. I was putting the new registration sticker on my car. So I used one of those razor blade scrapers to take off the old one. I put in a fresh blade, scraped off the old sticker, then set the blade on a towel that was sitting on the passenger seat. Then I forgot all about the damn thing. I came back later, opened the passenger door, and thought I was just grabbing the towel. Except that the scraper was kind of hidden in the towel, and my finger hit it just right, or just wrong I should say. So I took a clean slice off the tip. Damn thing bled like crazy. I can see why patients who take a daily aspirin like I do can bleed to death after a car wreck. I probably lost close to a pint of blood from this little cut."

"My God! So you went to the ER, I trust."

"Actually I didn't. There was really nothing to do for it, Pat. It's just going to have to heal by secondary intention. It just wasn't anything that could be sutured or grafted."

"Who determined that, and how did you stop the bleeding?"

"With lots of pressure. Trust me, Pat. This isn't that bad. I'll be able to see consults and post ops in the office Monday. I just have a finger cot on it right now. By mid week I'll probably be up to some simpler office surgeries, and I can be back in the OR by next Monday. Fortunately, it's on my left hand, the ring finger. But it will keep me from doing a full surgical scrub for a few days yet. Can you help me contact some patients and adjust Monday's schedule? I'm looking at it now and it really shouldn't be too bad making the adjustments. By the way, I see that ER follow-up still hasn't been scheduled, you know, the machete man. Did we send him a registered letter?"

"It was returned with a signature but he never did call to make a follow-up appointment. I know you really wanted to see his result, but he's impossible. I left at least three phone messages and followed up with the registered letter. Did you know that he had no medical insurance but he paid his bill in full? So I doubt that he's unhappy in any way. He just won't respond."

"I never even saw him for suture removal."

"I suppose those folks have their own network of doctors, sort of like a medical *consigliere*."

"Careful, Pat. Those are my folks you're talking about."

"Dr. Gianni, I don't expect you share much of anything with that patient, apart from a name that ends in a vowel. Now are you sure there's nothing else you need right now?"

"I'm sure, Pat. Thank you."

Once they finished, he picked up the phone again, this time to call Chet Pawlek's cell phone.

"Chet, it's Gianni. We have to talk."

"It's Sunday. What the hell is so important?"

"I had a visit, I guess you might call it that, from your pals the Catroni boys."

"Fucking bastards, Anthony. What the hell did they want with you, cocksuckers?"

"I'm at my office right now. No one else is here. I think you better come in right now."

GIANNI HEARD THE POUNDING on the door, four loud thumps, Chet's signature knock. He walked to the entrance and unlocked the door.

"What the fuck is going on," Chet bellowed.

Gianni walked back to his office with Chet bounding behind.

"You tell me," Gianni said.

Chet looked at the walls of Gianni's office, at the diplomas and a framed newspaper clipping that featured Dr. Gianni. "How did you ever get mixed up in this b-b-business? My business, I mean. Look at all these awards and shit."

"If I had known this would be part of the package, Chet, I would have just adopted some retired thoroughbred and kept him on a farm near my house in Westchester. No one told me I might lose a finger or two if I bought a race horse."

Chet picked up an antique surgical instrument from Gianni's desk, holding it in his large fat hands. "I could use something like this though, might come in handy," he said smiling.

Gianni took the finger cot off his ring finger and waved it at Chet, then pressed the fingers of both hands into a steeple and stared at him across the desk. "Listen to me Chet. Catroni told me to show you this. Some guy named Hector did it to me." He gestured again with the cut finger. "They told me to tell you that if Chiefly Endeavor doesn't die, then there are more fingers to go, mine and yours. They told me they didn't think you'd want that to happen to me."

Chet raised his voice, "You didn't go to the p-p-police, did you?"

"I didn't think it would do any good. Plus, it's not the sort of publicity I need for my practice right now. Mobster takes a slice off surgeon's finger! Great for business. I need that like a bull needs tits."

"Well you're sure as hell right about it not doing any good. These fucking bastards have no morals. You go to the police and next thing you know your wife shows up dead."

"Actually, they asked me about Janice, in a mocking way. Just to let me know they knew her name, I suppose."

Chet exploded again, "Jesus Christ, those mother fucking bastards."

"Why were you asking me those questions a while back, about equine influenza, and the equine herpes virus? Gianni said. Did you have a horse contract some viral illness?"

"No…I mean, well y-yeah, a while ago. All right, truth be told, they came to me a while back. I owe them some money. A lot of money, actually. And I can't pay it, not right now anyway. So they asked me about insurance and all. I mean, I thought about it, about something happening to the horse, but I would n-n-never do *anything* to that horse, never."

"Chet, so help me God, *if you ever* do anything to harm that horse, I will kill you. I may be a surgeon, but I'm also a hunter and a damn good marksman. I have a collection of rifles and some very accurate pistols too, like my 38 Special 1911. Believe me, I know how to use them. And believe me, I will protect that horse with the same vengeance that I would my family. I will hunt you down first and worry about the consequences later."

"Look Anthony, I'm sorry this all happened. I never in a million years thought you'd be dragged into this whole mess. This is my problem, and those bastards had no right…"

"So what do we do now?" Gianni interrupted.

"I have to think. I don't know. I'll have to speak with my advisors, you know. Did they say how long b-b-before…"

"Before what, Chet?"

"Well, before they'd be back."

"No, but I expect we'll hear. Clearly a dead horse is worth

more for them than a surgeon's finger. How much money do you owe them?"

"Five mill, give or take a little interest."

"How much can you get together?" Gianni asked.

"I can work this out, I promise. I don't want you involved. And nothing is going to happen to the h-h-horse, you have my word on that. I'll speak with my advisors and we'll work this out with those Catroni pricks."

"It better happen fast, Chet."

"It will, Anthony. Trust me, it will. I mean your nerves must be shot."

"I'm a fighter, Chet. My nerves are fine. But it better happen fast."

Chapter 18

Two weeks later

"Dr. Gianni, you have a call on line two, Mr. Duncker calling."

"Can you tell him I'll call him right back, please? I'm just finishing a report."

The receptionist buzzed him back a moment later. "Dr. Gianni, he says it's urgent. He asked if you were in surgery."

"Hello, Stu."

"Anthony, do you have some time? I'm afraid I have some terrible news. It's Chiefly Endeavor. I received a call from Midway earlier today. The night watchman found him in his stall early this morning. He died this morning, Anthony. I'm so sorry."

"How..."

"We don't know anything yet, I'm afraid. There will be an autopsy, of course. And a huge insurance investigation, no doubt. I plan to speak with the press in the morning. I'll get the news out to that Resnick chap who works with Associated Press.

I like his style, and I trust he'll be fair. And of course I'll let you talk directly with your old pal, Dr. Highet. He has some real concerns. Medically, I mean. He's a bit baffled by the whole thing, or so he led me to believe. I wish I knew more. You're the first of the partners I called. I know how attached you were to that horse."

"I'll call Highet," Gianni replied faintly. "Goodbye, Stu."

Gianni hung the receiver up and tapped his left hand on the desk. He heard the dull thump of his blunted ring finger on the wood and stopped when he felt the stinging still present in the healing digit.

He flipped open his Rolodex and dialed the number for Rood and Riddle, the world famous equine hospital in Lexington. He had meant to call his old college acquaintance for some time now, but never quite got around to it. Now it couldn't wait.

"Dr. Steven Highet, please. This is Dr. Anthony Gianni calling."

Highet came to the phone quickly. "Dr. Anthony Gianni, I can't believe it."

"Hello Steven. Do you know I've wanted to call you ever since I got into this crazy horse business and just never got around to it? And now…"

"I'm really sorry, Anthony. And we will get together and catch up on all the years. But this whole thing is just tragic and quite frankly, confusing to me right now."

"What in hell happened?" Gianni asked.

"I don't know, but I promise you, I intend to find out. About all I can tell you now is that I received a panicked call from the night watchman at Midway early this morning. It wasn't even light yet, but

I had started my rounds there and I was just two barns over when I got the call on my cell. So I literally ran to his stall and found him on the ground. Looked at first glance like he could have just been sleeping, but he had no pulse and he wasn't breathing. He'd been dead for some time, and there was no chance of resuscitation. The necropsy, or autopsy, is scheduled for tomorrow and we've ordered full toxicology screens. It's my case, Anthony, and believe me I'm going to be all over it."

"I loved that horse. Can we work together on this?"

"I intend to keep you informed every step of the way. Even Stu Duncker has said I can communicate with you primarily, which he doesn't often do. He usually likes to keep his partners just slightly stupid, from what I've seen. We normally have instructions to speak only with him. I guess he thinks your medical knowledge may come in handy here, and he does know we're old friends."

"Call me any time, Steven. I want to know what's going on, and I want to help in any way I can."

Gianni hung up the phone and stared out the window at nothing in particular. *Chester Pawlek. Could the stupid bastard have actually done it after all?*

Chapter 19

John Pawlek paused at the entrance to the Newark Division Office of the FBI. He had spent weeks rehearsing, mulling over how much information he was willing to give. He figured he could discover enough to put his father away for life. He also knew he had little to lose, having already rejected any ties to the family business. In his mind, he had abandoned his family ties long ago, though he and his father still spoke.

John Pawlek was not the stereotypic mafia kid. In fact, he was a bundle of contradictions. John was a voracious reader but a poor student. He hated his father's business associates, as Chet called them, but he loved to go target shooting with one of them, a man dubbed "Uncle Ralphie" by Chet.

John stood nearly six feet tall, with a muscular frame sculpted by years of weight training, but spoke with a soft, womanish voice. His voice sounded a lot like his mother's, with the same New Jersey accent; yet he was far more articulate than either of his parents.

His father often made fun of his effeminate voice, and his reading habits, too. Chet would stroll into John's room, pick up a novel he was reading and ask, "What's this, another girlie book?"

As much as he hated Chet, John still found it difficult to complete this act of betrayal. It would be completed with little sense of satisfaction or revenge. What motivated him and steadied him now was the recollection of that evening when he heard his father and mother talking about Chiefly Endeavor.

Al Hollis, the senior investigator on the Pawlek case, introduced himself and sat across the table from John. He was a shorter man who looked to be about forty, with a balding head and diminutive grey eyes that disappeared into his plump face. John thought he looked a little too soft for an FBI man, but still frightening. The office was plain, rather stark. John imagined that some really hardened criminals had sat in the same chair, as he readied himself for his own interrogation.

"First Mr. Pawlek, I want to thank you for coming in today; it shows a lot of courage and integrity on your part."

He hated to be called Mr. Pawlek by anyone, but he was too scared to say so right now. He nodded, his eyes shifting between Hollis and a photo on the wall. The photo depicted Hollis with the U.S. President. The President was shaking Hollis' hand and presenting some sort of award or plaque.

"You know your father is one of the suspects in the murder of that famous stallion he owned."

"Yes I do."

"And you're willing to help us?"

"Willing to try."

"I understand you and your father aren't exactly getting on very well right now."

"We never did, actually."

At that moment, a recollection took John back many years, breaking his concentration. He was in the Emergency Room at Englewood Hospital, his face battered and his lower lip cut. Fortunately, there had been no broken bones, and once again his mother had concocted the alibi—a scuffle with a friend, and no one suspected otherwise.

"So why are you willing to help us?" Hollis asked him for the second time.

John snapped to attention. "Because of the horse. I watched that horse grow up, watched him win the Preakness, went to visit him at the barns when he was stabled in Belmont or Saratoga. Some of the only good times I had with my father seemed to revolve around that horse."

"Do you think he could have had the horse killed somehow?"

"I know he talked about it."

"When?" the fed asked.

"A few weeks before the Chief died."

"What exactly did he say?"

"Something about the horse getting sick. That if someone could make the horse get sick, then he would get all the insurance money."

"Do you and your father still talk much?"

"Yeah, some."

"Does he ever talk about…business…in your presence?"

"Sometimes, usually if he's had a little too much to drink, which seems to happen a lot these days."

"So if he had, say, a little too much to drink some night, and you asked some questions about…business…you think he'd talk some?"

"Probably."

"And you told the agent in our Louisville office that you'd wear a wire for us, and record what he says?"

"Yeah, I did."

"John, I have to ask you again. Why are you willing to do this?"

"Because I want to find out myself if he was capable of killing that horse and if he did, he deserves to go to jail. And because I've been told about the witness protection program. About how I could go to a new state, and start a new life away from my father and all the lousy thugs he calls friends. I think I want that too."

"Okay then, I think we may have a deal in the works."

Chapter 20

"Equine herpes virus?" Gianni asked Highet. "That was the cause of death? I didn't know it could be fatal in the adult horse."

"It is typically a disease that can be fatal to newborn foals, same as in humans. But there have been a few deaths recently in adult horses. It causes a condition known as peracute pulmonary vasculitis, essentially a widespread vasculitis, especially in the lungs. It can literally kill a horse overnight, and that's what happened here."

"How in hell did he contract it? Gianni asked.

"Anthony, that's my concern. I don't think he acquired the virus by any natural mode of transmission."

"What?"

"He had been screened for the virus, so we know he wasn't a latent carrier. And there are no other sick horses, not at Midway, anyway."

"So how could it have occurred?"

"Look, I may be way out on a limb here, and this is still preliminary, but if the horse was susceptible, it wouldn't take much more than a nasal swab, or something saturated with secretions from an actively infected horse or foal."

"God Almighty, Steven, we need to meet soon. I haven't told you about some of the darker moments in my dealings with Chiefly Endeavor. I know at least three people who wanted that horse dead. I think I should fly down so we can meet face to face. Will you have some time this weekend?"

"I'll make time."

"I'll let you know the details as soon as I make my reservations. I'll probably reserve a room at the Griffin Gate in Lexington."

After he hung up the phone, he thought about calling Chet. *Not yet. I need to know a little more first.*

Chapter 21

The large sign at the exit to Lexington's Bluegrass Airport read:

Welcome to Lexington Kentucky
Sister City to Newmarket, England
County Kildaire, Ireland
Shinhidaka, Japan
Deauville, France

This listing was not just a passing reference to some of the world's greatest racing destinations. Lexington was part of Sister Cities International, a non-profit organization with a goal of fostering diplomacy between U.S. and international communities. Gianni knew this because of his involvement with a volunteer program that the New York City Department of Health had sponsored for one of its sister cities, Rome, Italy.

This was the heart of Bluegrass Country, the landscape dotted with magnificent thoroughbred farms. Driving down Route 60,

Gianni admired the red and white colors adorning the gates and the buildings of Calumet Farm. The white fences went on endlessly.

In the 1990s, when Calumet was under different ownership and financially troubled, it didn't appear as resplendent. That was the year when Alydar, one of Calumet's best-known stallions, had died under very mysterious conditions. Some felt that the horse had been murdered in order to recover insurance monies, though foul play was never proven and the insurance company ultimately paid more than $35 million.

Gianni had read several accounts of the story, like Ann Hagedorn Auerbach's *Wild Ride,* and he thought Alydar had in fact been murdered. Though Chiefly Endeavor was worth far less than Alydar at the time of his death, Gianni anticipated that the investigation surrounding Chiefly Endeavor would be more thorough. These were different times, a different horse and another farm.

He settled into his room at the Griffin Gate, showered and walked across the expansive lawn towards the Mansion, an adjacent restaurant in a two story, white antebellum mansion. On the open lawn, a boy was playing with a golden retriever. Gianni stopped to admire the dog and the retriever approached him, tail wagging with friendly enthusiasm. He paused and scratched the dog between the ears, then resumed his walk across the lawn.

He had asked for a table in the outdoor lounge area, expecting that his troika would have sufficient privacy. It was late in the afternoon, sunny, but too cool to expect anyone to ask for an outdoor perch. There would be no real crowd in any case. Keeneland's racetrack was closed and there were no sales or special events under way.

He sat facing the door that led from the bar out to the courtyard and continued to watch for Highet. The wind was unusually cool for early May, and he tightened the collar of his flight jacket.

He recognized Highet, a few pounds heavier, the face still youthful, weathered and suntanned. The purplish hemangioma around his left eye seemed to have faded some.

"Steven! I've just been reminiscing. I just calculated that it's been twenty-six years. We last met in Florida during our first winter vacation after finishing college."

"Right, and we went deep sea fishing with that lunatic out of Stuart," Highet said.

"Captain Wade! He's still at it. I almost went out with him last time I was in Florida, but the seas were too rough. Talk about a crazy bastard, but he knows how to catch fish."

"You look the same, really, Anthony."

"Oh sure!" Gianni replied. "I think maybe my patients are aging me faster than yours are aging you."

"I'm happy with my four-legged patients, but the hours are hell."

"We have a lot of catching up to do," Gianni said.

"I know," Highet said. "Terri Jones should be here any minute and she's anxious to talk to you. She needs any leads she can get at this point. You'll like her...big, ballsy brunette with a good sense of humor, easy to talk to. An ex-New Yorker, too."

Lt. Terri Jones walked out the door of the restaurant into the courtyard. She was a tall, dark-haired woman who looked more like a model than a cop, Gianni thought. Highet rose to make the introduction.

"Detective Terri Jones, this is Dr. Anthony Gianni."

She shook his hand firmly. When she spoke, a slight Long Island accent was still detectable. Gianni thought that her penetrating gaze, coupled with the accent and the handshake, declared a clear message: *Don't fuck with me.*

"Dr. Gianni, tell me if you will, how you got involved with the ponies?"

"I worked with thoroughbreds in the summers during high school and college. I did the hands-on, everyday stuff. I always loved the animals and the sport, so once I found myself with enough time and a little money, I looked at the various options for partnership."

"And you've only been with Bushmill, as an owner, I mean? Tell me about Stuart Garrison Duncker."

"Southern gentleman, very smooth. Very well regarded in the business. He's the patriarch of these racing partnerships, really."

"So you found yourself in a good one with Chiefly Endeavor?"

"I would say so."

"And who were the other partners?"

"Originally there were four. But after he won his second race, Chester Pawlek bought out two of the original partners. So that left me, Bradford Hill, Chester, and then Bushmill always keeps a minority interest and acts as the managing partner."

"Then the horse eventually went to Midway as a stallion. So who owned him at that point?"

"Chet owned half and Midway half. My ownership and Bushmill's were bought out by Midway, except for some breeding rights that we retained. And Bushmill continued to help with some of the promotion and PR work."

"Then all of the stud fees that the horse generates go to Midway and to Chester, or Chet you called him. Are you friends with Chet?"

"We're not friends." Gianni paused and Lt. Jones remained silent, as if she expected him to say more.

"Actually, I despise Chester. I was forced into partnership with him because he bought out the other partners in Chiefly Endeavor. In a way, though, I suppose I also pity him. I think he may be one of those people who's trapped in a life he can't stand. And he worked so goddamn hard to get it. Do you know anyone like that, Detective?"

She seemed a bit surprised by the question and the candor. "I suppose I do, Doctor."

Gianni was thinking of his wife, Janice, thinking how she too had wanted a certain lifestyle so badly, and now that she had it, it brought her no real happiness or fulfillment.

Terri Jones looked intently at Gianni. She waited awhile before she resumed her questioning. "So the only connection you had to the horse once he was at Midway was the breeding rights, worth how much?"

"Forty thousand per year. I can use them or I can sell them to a breeder."

"Did you maintain any kind of insurance connected to the horse?"

"Not once he stopped racing. The sole beneficiaries now are Midway and Chester."

"Dr. Highet told me you were willing to talk to me because you said you know that three people wanted the horse dead. Who are those three and why would they want to kill the horse?"

"Chet for one, because he is in deep financial trouble. A guy named Sal Catroni, because Chet owed him a large sum of cash that he seemingly couldn't pay. And an accomplice of Catroni's whom I only know as Hector. They work together."

"How about the folks at Midway? They obviously stand to gain once the insurance money comes through?"

"Not at all. This is a huge net loss for them, as far as I can see. They are a solid operation with many good stallions and good cash flows. Chiefly Endeavor was just getting started and stood to generate huge earnings. Plus, the negative press is already killing them, the fact that a young, presumably healthy stud dies on their farm. That certainly won't help their future business."

"You should also know that I am working in cooperation with the FBI on this case," she said. "They may want to speak with you at some point as well."

"That's fine. I want to see the murderer of that horse put away for life."

"We don't know yet if the horse was murdered, Doctor."

"Well what's your hunch?" Gianni asked.

"I don't work from hunches. You've given me three possibilities to investigate."

Gianni said, "I just think that one or more of them are involved. Dr. Highet doesn't think the horse died a natural death and I agree."

She said, "So maybe we're dealing with some random, deranged, horse slayer. Like in the play, *Equus*. My only point here is that all possibilities are still on the table."

"Detective, *anyone* that wanted to kill that horse was deranged," Gianni said.

Highet stood up and led the way through the courtyard, back inside and through the bar. Gianni continued talking to Terri Jones

116

and didn't notice the man sitting at the bar. He sat alone at one end, watching the television above the bar. He wore a baseball cap with the logo of Churchill Downs and large wraparound sunglasses. After the trio walked past him, he turned to consider them. On the right side of his face was a long vertical scar, at least six inches in length.

Chapter 22

Lexington, KY

Joe Travers, the general manager at Midway Farm, and Ryan Fischer were walking down one of the shedrows when Ryan paused at a stall where a large, thick-necked horse had his jaw around the edge of the stall window.

"Cribber," Travers said. "Likes to chew things. And when he grunts like that he's also swallowing air, which can be dangerous for some horses. So we always want to be sure the cribbers are eating okay. Plus, he's a Dynaformer."

"A what?" Ryan said, petting the sleek black head.

"A Dynaformer," Travers said, as the horse snapped his powerful jaw in the direction of Ryan's outstretched hand.

"Jesus! I thought you said you've been around horses. His sire… his papa was the great Dynaformer, which means he can be pretty rough on the mares, and it means he'll bite your goddamn hand off if you let him. So keep your hands to yourself. He doesn't like it when you try to pet him. Ask my foreman, Arturo, to tell you the story he heard from his brother. His brother worked with the big horse himself. As the story goes, Dynaformer once bit three fingers off some poor groom. Swallowed them in one gulp too, never to be seen again."

"Jesus…I have been around horses though," Ryan said.

"These are thoroughbred race horses. They're not your average goddamn pets. Are you sure you want this job?"

"I'm sure."

"You know, ninety percent of our grooms and handlers are Mexican. You speak any Spanish?"

"A little."

"Can you get along with a bunch of hot-headed Mexicans?"

"Why wouldn't I?"

"Things are tense around here right now. Imagine you read about the death of our prized stallion?

"Chiefly Endeavor," Ryan replied.

"Well I guess you read the papers, even if you don't know shit about horses.

I don't know, college boy. Why do you want this job anyway? Pay's not great."

"I really need to make some extra money this summer. Plus, I know you need the extra help, what with the immigration crackdown and all. And the whole racing thing fascinates me."

"Fascinates you, eh! Okay, but just remember there ain't a goddamn Mexican in this barn who knows what the hell fascinate is. So I suggest you keep it real simple, or better yet, brush up on your Spanish, college boy."

"Does that mean I'm hired?"

"That means I'm giving you a chance. We'll both know in a

week if it's going to work. Be here tomorrow at 6:30 sharp, ready to work your ass off."

TAKING HIS CUES from some of the grooms he encountered during his interview, Ryan showed up the next day dressed in his rattiest pair of jeans, work boots and a tee shirt. That attire wasn't all that different from Ryan Fischer's everyday dress at Colby College.

"Ryan, meet Arturo Lopez. Lopey is one of my best men, been with me for years—except for the few times he returned to visit his family back in Mexico. Lopey, you keep an eye on things here while I take a garbage run with Ryan. Then next week he can do it all by his lonesome."

"Hola," Ryan said.

"Hello, Ryan." Lopey replied with a heavy Spanish accent. He had thick, dark hair gathered into a pony tail under his baseball cap. The grey cap had "Las Vegas" written across the front in large blue letters.

Ryan wondered if the English reply was a testament to his poor dialect, so he tried again. "Como esta?"

"Not bad, you?"

Okay, so maybe my Spanish sucks, Ryan thought.

"Hey Ryan, get in the truck!" Travers yelled.

For the next half hour they went barn to barn loading garbage-filled bins onto the long-bed pickup truck, then drove to the town dump. They drove to the back end of the landfill, where raw, non-recyclable refuse was piled high in three towering mounds. The stench was strong. As they began emptying the cans, they were greeted by three of the strangest looking creatures Ryan had ever laid eyes on.

Each looked to be around fifty— though with Kentucky hill folks, it's often difficult to tell.

There were two men and a woman. The woman had long grey and black hair hanging in a tangled mess around her wrinkled face and neck. One of the men was much shorter than the other, and he had on a worn-out fedora that sat on the back of his head. His face was round and plump, his body short and squat.

Travers saw Ryan's puzzled look. "That's Crow and Juicy. And over there is Zoom."

Zoom was the tallest of the lot, more wrinkled and even dirtier looking than Crow. He joined the other two as they all came closer to the truck and began to rummage through the piles, paying special attention to what was thrown off the truck.

Crow, Juicy, Zoom. He has to be kidding, Ryan thought. *This has to be some sort of first day initiation prank for college boy.*

The old woman came to the edge of the pickup and reached in to grab a worn-out bridle from the end of the truck bed. Ryan caught a glimpse of her hand, blackened with weeks of unwashed grime, nails curled and irregular, some nearly an inch long. Her small dark eyes were deeply set and framed by dirty, wrinkled skin. She grabbed her treasure and scowled at Ryan.

No, this was no joke; those hands were real, and she did look like a crow, claws and all. She clutched the bridle in her hand, turned her hunched shoulders and slowly headed back towards home. Home was an abandoned yellow school bus, propped up on cinder blocks, with shreds of curtain on some of the windows. Outside the bus were a few half-dead potted plants placed amidst the weeds and sand.

"Hey, you working or not," Travers yelled, reminding Ryan

that he had probably ceased all movement for a short time while he watched Crow trudge on homeward.

Once the truck was emptied, Ryan slowly walked back to the cab, still hypnotized by the sight of the two men, who remained in the garbage piles.

"What's wrong, college boy?" Travers asked as they drove out.

"Nothing, I guess. Just that Zoom dude, he looks like one mean bastard."

"Don't expect any of them to be friendly, and don't let them ever hear you say the nicknames: Crow…Juicy…Zoom. I don't even know their real names, town folks gave them those names and they stuck. Heard a kid once called the lady "Crow" by mistake in the Midway General Store and Zoom about scared the kid half to death, threatened to kill the poor son of a bitch."

"They live in that bus, all three of them?"

"For as long as I can remember. Town pays them something, peanuts I'm sure, to maintain the dump. Benefits must be okay, though. They keep what they want and sell the rest, I guess. Story has it that Crow and Juicy are common law husband and wife. And Zoom, well, I'm not really sure how he fits in."

"Is there a bathroom or running water in that thing?" Ryan asked.

"Doubt it, but the dump has water."

"Why do you suppose Crow grabbed that bridle out of the truck?"

"How the hell should I know? Probably to hang in her kitchen for a goddamn decoration."

"Did you see Zoom snap it out of her hand a little later?" Ryan asked.

"Zoom is the meanest of the three, meaner and stranger than he looks even. You know he was picked up outside the main gate of the farm the same day our young stallion was found dead. The local cops dragged him in and grilled him for a few hours, but I don't think they came up with anything. Don't know for sure if the feds have looked at him yet; they're on the case too. Still, he's one weird bastard. You'll make this run yourself next week. Just don't plan any trips after dark. If the black bears don't kill you at night, Zoom just might."

Chapter 23

John Pawlek felt empowered by the wire he concealed under his shirt. Instructed by the federal agents, he was confident in his ability to conceal it from his father. Once activated, it would record his father's confessions, just like the ones John had mentally recorded when he would sit in the hallway down from his parents' room.

He planned the visit to his home in northern New Jersey in the early evening. Such visits were becoming less common since John had begun his freshman year at Rutgers, but an evening visit would not be totally unexpected either. Usually John stopped to see his mother, though tonight he knew she was still visiting her sister in Savannah. Chet, more likely than not, would be half in the bag by six in the evening, having gorged himself with leftovers and booze.

Pulling through the stone markers at the end of the driveway, John felt a blend of that familiar sense of dread and anger. He announced his arrival with two rings of the bell, another habit he had acquired since leaving home. He no longer considered it his home. He wouldn't just walk in, or use the keys that were still on his keychain, the ones that opened the double deadbolt locks. Normally his mother would answer and then Chet would bellow out, *"Jesus Christ, you're our son. You don't need to ring the goddamn doorbell, John."* Tonight there was no answer, so he let himself in with the keys.

Shit, I hope he's not already passed out on the couch. If he is, I'll just wake the old bastard up, and he'll probably babble on even more than usual.

He wasn't on the couch, so John walked through the kitchen and looked out the glass doors at the lagoon-shaped swimming pool. He thought about some of the better days, the earlier times with his father when they first had the pool built. Did he actually love his father then, or was he just too young to know any better? Probably the latter, because what he remembered most right now were all of the sadistic beatings, the countless trips to the Emergency Room, and the stories that always had to be told to cover up the truth. His mother had become a master at that.

He called out, "Dad? It's me. Are you here?"

The Mercedes wasn't in the garage, so he wondered if his father was out somewhere. But the alarm wasn't on. More likely, his mother drove the Mercedes to the airport and left it.

The house was incredibly quiet. John thought about a quote he had read for a journalism class, a quote from Fran Liebowitz. Something about how money can buy privacy...and silence. When you walk into the home of a rich person, it is invariably quiet. But if you don't have money, your walls are thinner, your neighbors closer, and your house is noisier.

Then he thought of the backstretch at Belmont Park, a place he loved to visit. The backstretch huts were invariably noisy. John looked at the foyer floor, with its expensive tiles that had been imported from Italy. He thought of his father's wealth and how it had been acquired. How many people had been abused or actually killed? He remembered how his father mistreated all the little people who were so important to his success in the racing business, one of his few legitimate business ventures.

"Dad? Where are you?" He was on a tour of the house now, walking upstairs, looking in the various rooms. "Dad?" Peeking in the upstairs den, he smelled the faint odor of cigar smoke, but still heard no answer.

It has to be too early for him to be passed out on the bed. He walked into the master bedroom and noticed a stepladder in the large walk-in closet. The ladder was lined up to a trap door that opened into the attic. A faint light shone through the opening into the darkened closet.

"Dad? What the hell are you doing up there?"

No answer. Now he could hear a creaking sound, like an old wooden floor under footsteps, or like the sound of rafters creaking with the wind.

He climbed the stepladder partway then boosted himself up the rest of the way into the attic crawl space. A single bulb lit the entire expanse. Old furniture and cardboard boxes sat on the wood planking near the trap door. Further down it was darker and more difficult to see clearly. The creaking seemed louder. Where the wood planking ended, the roof line became steeper. It was dark enough here that John could see light from outside filtering through the soffit vents. His eyes then moved from the vents, up the rafters on the underside of the roof.

He looked in the direction of the creaking sound and saw movement…back and forth, with the creaks, swaying. His eyes adjusted to the darkness at that end. A rope hung from the rafters. A body, dangling from the rope, lifeless. John gasped in horror and quickly turned his head away from the hanging corpse.

Chapter 24

Ryan had made enough trips to the dump, at varying times, so he figured he had a reasonable idea of the daily routines of Crow, Juicy and Zoom. The heaviest traffic into the landfill came from early morning through early afternoon. Any time a truck would come in, the trio would meander over in the direction of the truck to check out their wares. If enough traffic came in, they would be occupied for some time and would be away from their bus. Ryan knew he had to get a closer look at their roost.

So he figured mid-day, in the midst of the heaviest traffic, he'd likely have his best chance. It would also have to fall on one of his days off, as Travers left him little leeway for goofing off. He worked a six day week, and his day off could fall on any given day. A weekday would be best, no doubt.

It was a Thursday in August, scorching hot, when Ryan set out in his own car for the landfill. He selected an inconspicuous spot about a half mile down the county road where he could pull his vehicle into a clearing off to the side. Then he could climb the fence a hundred feet from the main gate so he wouldn't be noticed. He had scoped out a path from there, through a lightly wooded area, which would give him an entry to the rear of the school bus. If he saw the three scavengers in the refuse piles, then he would assume the coast was clear.

At the rear of the bus, Ryan saw several tall piles of newspapers and magazines, neatly piled against the rear of the bus, right up to the level of the bus windows. Were they being sorted for recycling by one of his three friends? Not likely, as the paper recyclables were collected and deposited in a separate area of the landfill, he knew. On top of one of the stacks was a *Blood Horse Magazine*, the trade journal. He picked it up and noted that it was several months old. He fingered through the next half dozen or so in the pile. They were all issues of *Blood Horse*, all slightly dated, but all in the current calendar year. On top of the adjacent pile was a *Daily Racing Form*, and he quickly determined that, like the other pile, this one contained a stack of slightly dated papers, all of them *Racing Forms*. Did the school bus residents collect them and save them for reading? More likely they kept them to start kindling wood on fire, or for cleaning or some other utilitarian function. But they seemed to be perfectly sorted, which was odd.

Ryan stood on his toes in order to be able to peek into one of the windows at the rear of the bus. The bus had been gutted and old mattresses were on the floor, collected from someone's trash, no doubt. He stretched his neck to look down the bus at a tiny table with three chairs, then he suddenly felt something tighten on his neck. He fell to the ground, his shirt collar still held tight around his neck, half choking him. He struggled to turn his head and saw that it was Zoom who gripped his collar and now had a boot to Ryan's spine as he pulled the collar even tighter. Ryan looked up into the bug-eyed gaze of a crazy man.

"What the hell are YOU doin here, KID?"

"If you let me go I can talk," Ryan sputtered.

"I'll let you go, then if you DON'T talk, I'll kill you right here, ya bastard." He spoke with the distinctive dialect of a southern hillbilly.

He released the hold on Ryan's collar, throwing him onto his back.

"Now get up! What the hell ya doing here, boy?"

"I'm sorry, mister. I'm new here and just trying to find my way around. I work at one of the horse farms and I have to come here sometimes, and I thought maybe this is where the newspapers go…Is this where they go? I just don't want any trouble, mister."

"Where's your truck, KID?"

"I…I don't have it today. Had my car out today for a ride, and it was acting up in this heat. So I left it down the road to cool down, then walked up here to see if I could drum up some water and a jug, in case it happens again. And, well, I just got to looking around a bit. That's all, honest."

"What farm you working at?"

"Midway."

Zoom's temperament seemed to change a bit now, softened either by the young boy's pleadings, or perhaps by the mention of Midway.

"Whadya do there at Midway?"

"Whatever. Groom. Walker. Drive here sometimes."

"How often you come HERE now?"

"Once a week, usually." Ryan relaxed now, feeling he was more in control of his circumstance once again.

"Guess you don't look like too bad a kid. Come here now."

Zoom walked around to the front of the bus, to where an emergency exit had been cut wider to serve as an entryway. Ryan hesitated for a moment, then slowly followed. Zoom went inside and came out with a gallon plastic jug.

"Go over there," he said, pointing across the sandy field. "There's a spigot over there. Fill it up then you better get your car to a station. Pure water may get you a few miles, but if your engine's hot, you'll need a bottle of antifreeze. Same as I need when it gets a little hot or cold, if you know what I mean."

"Yeah, I know," Ryan said with a forced laugh.

"What's your name kid?"

"Ryan."

The man looked up and down at the boy. He smiled, displaying a crooked row of half-rotten teeth. "I'm Mahlon. Call me Mahlon."

Chapter 25

Detective Henry Chang was a large, muscular man, well over six feet tall. His friends would often goad him, saying he was the largest Chinese man they had ever seen. He had a low, resonant voice and a gentle demeanor. He took Delores Pawlek's hand. "My condolences, Mrs. Pawlek. Do you have someone with you?"

"No, I'll be fine."

"Come with me, then."

They entered the morgue together and Chang led her to a steel table. When the face was uncovered, her eyes widened. She considered the corpse, its face grey and waxy looking, then looked across at the detective.

"Oh my God! It's not him."

"What?"

"It's not him, Detective. This is not my husband."

"But when your son called—"

"My son was in shock. He called me before he called the police.

He was hysterical, and he couldn't force himself to look at the body for more than an instant. It was hanging from the rafters in a dark attic, for God's sake."

"But you said your husband left a suicide note?"

"I have it with me."

"All right. Let's go somewhere we can talk."

Chang dialed the number for Dr. Laurie Simmons in the office of the chief medical examiner. "Dr. Simmons, Henry Chang. We have no I.D. on the hanging. I want to know the minute you have the toxicology and cause of death. This case gets stranger by the minute. I'll check with missing persons, but we'll need complete dental forensics in any case." After he hung up, he said, "We can walk to my office from here."

The air outside was thick and steamy. Sweat ran down the sides of Henry Chang's face. As they entered his office on the second floor of the Englewood Police Department, he turned the air conditioner fan on high, reached into his suit coat pocket and wiped his face and his huge bald head with a handkerchief.

The small room smelled of cheap cologne and body odor. Delores sat across from Chang and passed the letter to him. Chang read it silently.

When you read this I will be gone, to a better place I hope. I want you to know that I will always love you and I will always love John, even if I didn't always show it. You both meant more to me than anything in this world.

>*With all my love,*

>*Chester*

"Would you have expected more than this, Mrs. Pawlek?"

"From my husband? No, he only does short stories. A man of few words."

"Where and when did you find the note?"

"It was on our kitchen table, tucked under a plate. I found it as soon as I came back home."

"You were in Savannah?"

As she spoke, she glanced down at one shoulder, then at the other and repeatedly brushed off her knit dress with the back of her fingers. "I was visiting my sister. As soon as John called me I got on the first plane, which wasn't until the following morning. I called the police myself; John was such a wreck, you know."

"Who knew that you were out of town?"

"I don't know. My husband and my son, obviously. And a couple of my girlfriends."

"Do you have any idea who the other man was, the body we just viewed?"

"No."

"Now why…and how…would a two hundred pound man end up hanging in your attic? Let's say your husband wanted to simply escape somewhere. I know that he has been under investigation for a crime in Kentucky. If he staged his own suicide, and actually killed another man as a decoy, he clearly would have needed help getting the body up there. Not a problem for your husband, I'm sure. But why go to all that trouble? Why not just run? I'm sure he has plenty of resources to make that happen. Of course, knowing that you were away, I imagine he figured he had several days before anyone would even find the body. Your husband has killed before, hasn't he, Mrs. Pawlek?"

"Detective, I would like to call my lawyer."

"You can call your lawyer. Now we'll need to dust your bedroom and attic for prints, though I doubt he'd leave that trail. Mrs. Pawlek, how many cars does your family own?"

"Two, the one I drove today and one other."

"And where is the other one?"

"I don't know. That's another mystery. It's not in the garage."

"Whose name is the other car registered under?"

"My husband's."

"You could save us a little time if you could tell me the make, model and plate number."

"It's a red Mercedes SL. You can't miss it. The license plate says: 'RACEDAY.'"

"Mrs. Pawlek, do you think your husband is alive?"

"I'd like to call my lawyer now."

Chapter 26

Gianni studied the photograph on his desk. It was a picture of a seventeen-year-old boy from the island of St. Lucia. The tip of the boy's nose had been bitten off by a rat, leaving a hideous defect. It was one of the cases that Gianni would be asked to manage during his upcoming mission.

As he tried to focus on planning the surgery for the case, he was continually distracted. He thought of Chet, whom he had been trying to contact for days, and to no avail. Was Chet trying to ditch him for good, possibly because Chet *did* have something to do with his stallion's death? He wondered about Highet, and why he had no additional information on the demise of Chiefly Endeavor. Gianni knew he needed to get to Lexington again, and soon.

A surge of anxiety caught Gianni off guard. He set the photograph aside for a moment, distracted by the recollection of a bizarre, disturbing dream he had during a restless night earlier that week.

He dreamt that he was back in his surgical residency in Queens, NY. He was a patient in a hospital room and his roommate was an amputee, a man named Clem, someone Gianni actually knew when he was a first year resident there. Clem was a double-amputee who had lost both legs to frostbite, living on the streets of Jamaica, NY. He had a simple wooden cart on wheels, and he would occasionally wheel himself into the men's room on the first floor of the hospital, especially during the winter months. Gianni remembered him washing up at one of the low sinks, or just sleeping in a corner by the urinals, usually with a bottle in his hand. Sometimes they would speak briefly, or else Gianni just let him be. Unlike some of the other house officers, who would tend to feel uneasy and call Security, Gianni never wanted to turn poor Clem in. He knew that on a good day, Security might bring him to the ER. On a bad one, they might just move Clem outside again.

In his dream, Gianni and Clem were talking when Sal Catroni entered the hospital room, dressed like a doctor, with a long white coat and a surgical headlight on his head. He was carrying an orthopedic surgical saw in one hand and a gun in the other. He said he was there to adjust Gianni's legs, so they would look more like Clem's. Then he started the saw, only now it looked and sounded like a chain saw instead of the surgical saw. When the saw started up, Gianni woke from the dream with a gasp, his heart racing.

After recalling the dream, Gianni tried to concentrate on the photograph again and to plan his approach for creating a nasal tip on the boy in St. Lucia. He would need to take some cartilage from the ear, and obtain some soft tissue covering from a flap rotated into the nasal area, probably from the forehead or cheek area. He knew that he could not accomplish everything in one surgery and that another surgeon on a subsequent mission would likely have to take over.

His thoughts drifted again, this time to his decision to enter the field of plastic and reconstructive surgery many years back. He was drawn to the specialty because of a genuine desire to treat the most disfiguring defects—the severe congenital facial deformities, burn victims and the like. Yet in his current practice, he saw those patients only occasionally. Still, it had been *his* decision to enter private practice rather than academic medicine, where the more major deformities were usually treated.

Wasn't that where his focus should be, on his patients and his craft? Why was he even in this damn horse business at all? Then he recalled working the farm in his youth, turning the young foals out to pasture, alongside their mothers. It was breathtaking to see a newborn foal stand for the first time on its spindly legs, or take that first awkward but beautiful run around the paddock, growing stronger and more graceful with each stride. Duncker had always said you have to love the sport, and the animals. Gianni did, and Chiefly Endeavor had been his favorite.

He worried about having to leave the country in the midst of everything else that was going on with the stallion, the threats to himself or potentially to Janice, and his inability to contact Chet. Still, he knew that he had to honor the commitment. He wondered if on some level, he actually wanted to escape. Regardless, he knew he had to get back to Kentucky again to see Highet and to find out more about Chiefly Endeavor. And he had to do it before he left for the island of St. Lucia.

Chapter 27

Ryan survived the first few weeks, including his ordeal with Zoom, whom he now knew as Mahlon. He had managed to impress Travers with his dependability and willingness to do whatever he was asked. He especially looked forward to the days like today when he would be asked to accompany Dr. Highet on his rounds.

"Hold him up close by the halter, not just the lead shank," Highet cautioned Ryan as the long tube went through the horse's gigantic nostril, passing on down the airway. "A lot of these horses are bleeders, which means when they over-exert they may get pulmonary edema, swelling in the lungs. The pressure of that swelling can push blood into the airway spaces. In a couple minutes, we can see exactly what's going on down there. A very useful instrument, this is."

"Travers said you vets crank these things out just to make money."

Highet's upper lip tightened. "Oh he did, did he? Well Travers doesn't know shit. First of all, a trainer has to ask me to scope their horse, and Travers should know that perfectly well. I do this because I'm asked to do it. Second, and I don't give a damn if Travers ever understands this, but I want you to. I didn't go into this profession just to make a lot of money. Sure, the pay is great, but it's not the main thing with me."

They were three stalls down now and onto the next scoping as Highet continued his story. "From the time I was a little kid, we always made a thing out of watching the Triple Crown races. My family had one of those big screen televisions, nothing like today's version, but pretty fancy for Malone, NY in those days. So half the neighborhood would come over, and we'd all throw a dollar or two into a pot and try to pick a winner. It was great fun and I always loved the horses…loved riding them and loved watching them. But…there were a few times when I saw horses injured, and one time I'll always remember when they had to put a horse down. This square van drove out on the track like a big overgrown hearse, a curtain went up so the crowd couldn't see, and the horse's life ended right there on the track. I remember always wanting to know why the horse had to die. I'd ask my parents but never got a very good answer. So from the time I was a little kid, I thought that if I became a vet, I could save some of those horses. Corny but true."

"That's cool. You know," Ryan continued, "I haven't told anyone here about this, but I think I may want to be a vet too."

Highet's expression softened some. "No kidding. What's your major?"

"Psych, but I'm taking all the premed type courses I'd need for vet school. I just finished Vertebrate Anatomy last semester and got an A+."

"Congratulations."

"So, Dr. Highet, you never really wanted to do anything else? Are you still glad you became a vet?"

"It's really hard work. The hours are ridiculous sometimes. I left my house at 5 a.m. this morning and probably won't be home until 8 p.m. tonight. Those hours nearly broke up my marriage. For the first ten years of my daughter's life, the grooms around the barn probably knew me better than she did. But yeah, it's all I ever wanted to do, and it's all I want to do now. Except maybe to own a good racehorse myself some day. So are you sure you want to be a vet? I don't mean to scare you off, you know."

"I really think I do, and I understand what it will take to get there. Even this summer, Travers has to throw me out of here after ten hours, and I only get paid for eight, and paid peanuts at that. There's a reason I'm one of the few grooms here with totally legal papers."

Highet laughed. "I know, and that's another long story."

"What about that horse, Chiefly Endeavor?" Ryan asked.

"The Chief...sometimes we do all we can and they still die, Ryan."

Ryan took a deep breath. "I think I know something about Chiefly Endeavor."

They were done with rounds in Barn 5, and Highet clutched his instruments to his chest and looked directly at Ryan. "Like what?" he asked. He was already heading towards his truck as he spoke.

"Like Zoom, that weird guy at the dump," Ryan said.

"What the hell would Zoom have to do with a million dollar stallion?"

"Well, Travers told me they found him outside the farm

gates the morning Chief died. And since I found that out, I've been snooping around a little on my own."

"Look, Ryan. I've got a schedule to keep. You're really good help, and I'm going to ask Travers to have you assist me whenever I'm here."

"Great. Thanks, Doc." He appreciated the vote of confidence for his horse handling, even though Highet had quickly dismissed his detective skills. But he would have other chances.

Chapter 28

On Thursdays, Ryan Fischer was expected to make his run to the dump, bringing with him the bins of garbage from his assigned barns. It was close to noon when he drove into the landfill. Crow, Juicy and Zoom were nowhere to be seen.

He drove to the piles near the back and had nearly finished emptying the bins when Zoom emerged from the school bus.

"Hey, feller," he said. "Hot one today, ain't it?"

"Yeah, I'm dying in this heat."

"Want a cool one?" Zoom asked.

"A cool one?"

"Beer," Zoom said. "Nice cool beer."

Ryan knew that the last thing he should be doing is following Zoom into that decrepit bus to slug down a beer. Yet, he remained incredibly curious about the trio. He had to learn more about them and about the racing papers they kept neatly stacked behind the bus. He had seen Zoom mellow at the mention of Midway Farm and wanted to know why. He also knew that Travers would expect him back before long, so there was little time.

"Got any soda?" Ryan asked.

"Soda? You pussy," Zoom said.

"I don't want to get fired."

"All right boy. I'll get you some soda. Move your truck over by the shack."

Ryan drove the truck to the front of the bus and Zoom walked up behind him. Ryan had been working with his shirt off in the hot sun, and Zoom put his hand on Ryan's well-muscled back. He rubbed it in a short circular motion near the nape of his neck.

"Come on," he said. "I'll get you a nice cool one."

Inside the school bus, an acrid smell burned Ryan's nose. He resisted the instinct to cover his face and mouth. Crow and Juicy sat at a small round table. They were eating something out of a can. Ryan couldn't discern what it was, but he couldn't help noticing Crow's long, curled dirty nails as they dug into the can and shoveled food into her wrinkled mouth. *Holy shit. Lunch time.*

Zoom bent over a carton and took out a can of grape soda. He handed it to Ryan and yelled over to the table, "We got any ice left in the box?"

Fearing it might be Crow who would retrieve it, Ryan said, "I'll take it just like this. Thanks." Wafts of foul air continued to drift his way.

Crow and Juicy looked up from the table and stared at Ryan.

"He ain't no fucking ghost. Name's Ryan. He works at Midway," Zoom said.

Crow and Juicy continued to stare.

Ryan opened the can of soda and took a sip. It seemed like a long silence before he spoke again. "The other day when I was looking for the paper recyclables, I saw those two piles out back. I figured they couldn't be the recyclables because there were only two types of papers and they seemed to be all organized. Do you keep those to read yourself?"

"Hell no. I barely read at all. And those dumb bastards over at the table, they can't read shit."

Crow glared back at Zoom and Juicy spoke for the first time. "Fuck you. I can read some."

Zoom answered Ryan. "I save the papers for the hermit."

"The hermit?"

"Yeah. Lives about thirty miles or so due east of here, towards Clay City. In the woods, middle of nowhere. Weird old goat. There's a rumor he used to be some rich, famous guy. Taught at a college or something. Owned some horses too, I heard. Don't know if it's true, but he don't look to me like he ever owned nothing but that hut he lives in. Like me I guess, not like any rich man far as I can tell."

Ryan drank more of the soda.

"Anyway, pays me ten dollars to collect up the newspapers and magazines. Only wants those two kinds, though. He'll come here once every couple weeks, sort through and decide what he wants. Stuffs them into these old backpacks, many as he can, then heads on home."

Ryan wiped his mouth with the back of his hand. "Any idea what he does with them?"

"Don't know. Just loads them two backpacks and then rides his bike back home. It's thirty miles at least, and the last few miles I know he can't ride that bike, because there's too much woods. Only other time I know of when he comes out is to go to market outside of Lexington once or twice a month. Same thing, he comes in on the bike, packs up some canned stuff mostly, then he's gone. Nobody knows much about the hermit. He won't talk much."

"What's his name?" Ryan asked.

"Wayne. Don't even know his last name, just Wayne."

"You want some lunch with that soda?" Zoom asked.

"I really need to get going back to Midway."

"Well, don't work too hard. It's going to be a really hot one, you know." When he followed Ryan out of the bus, his face was close enough for Ryan to smell his sour breath, then Ryan felt a grimy hand rubbing his shirtless back as Zoom walked alongside him.

Chapter 29

"Good morning, Detective Jones. My name is Henry Chang and I'm with the Englewood Police Department. I'd like to speak with you about Chester Pawlek."

She shifted the phone to the opposite ear, "Yes?"

"I'm sure you know how complicated and wide-reaching this whole case has become."

"The feds told me you were in charge of the investigation surrounding the disappearance of Pawlek," she said. "I've been expecting your call."

"It's not just his disappearance," Chang said. "I'm also in charge of the murder investigation. You are aware of the hanging?"

"Yes. Do they have a positive I.D.?"

"His name was Servino, Paulie Servino. He was a relatively low-level mafioso who apparently made the fatal mistake. He pissed off the boss."

"You mean Chet?"

"Yeah. Their fights had become pretty public lately. It seems Paulie thought he should be getting a bigger piece of the action. He was a soldier long before Chet arrived on the scene."

Jones opened the file cabinet beside her desk and retrieved a file. "Why would he go to all that extra effort? Why not just shoot the guy in the head?"

"This is the Mafia, Detective Jones. These guys will make that extra effort if it means something to them personally. They'll take the time to chop a body into little pieces and pack the pieces neatly in a bunch of plastic bags. Sure, they'll walk into a crowded barber shop and blow some bastard away in the middle of a haircut, but they can also make it look like a man decided to jump out of a hotel window and end his happy life without the slightest sign of struggle. They will take the extra step if it suits their vision of how the man should die."

Chang continued, "In my years of investigating organized crime I've seen some very creative killing. I recall a case where all the hit man did was bump into his mark in a crowded bar, accidentally spilling his drink. Only the drink was actually cyanide. It seeped into the poor bastard's skin, eventually killing him, and no one knew why he died until the hit man eventually confessed, years later. If they want it quicker, or more direct, then they dump the cyanide directly into the poor sap's drink."

Thumbing through the file she had retrieved, Jones paused to look at photographs of Chester Pawlek and Anthony Gianni. "So what did the tox screen reveal here?" she asked.

"Positive for insulin. The levels were sky high. Shades of Claus von Bulow."

"And the cause of death?"

"Acute insulin toxicity."

Jones leaned back in her chair. "So they injected him first, then somehow dragged the body up and hung it from the rafters. Then in the midst of all the confusion, Chet got some extra time to make his end run to wherever, plus he's hung one of his enemies in his own attic as a little added bonus. Pretty damn circuitous, and the insulin part, does that really sound like a mob hit to you? Was this Servino a diabetic?"

"He wasn't. Maybe Chet had some medical advice for that part. Maybe we need to talk with your surgeon friend."

"Oh come on. What would Dr. Gianni stand to gain from killing some little known mobster?"

"Maybe he didn't have a choice. Chet made him an offer."

"Well, you can certainly talk to him, but I don't think Anthony Gianni is one to be easily intimidated. He hated Pawlek. I'm afraid that's where your theory breaks down, as far as I'm concerned."

"Maybe, but my theory certainly doesn't depend on Gianni being involved. The facts of the overdose and the hanging speak for themselves. I mean he hung the bastard in his own damn house. I just don't want to exclude any parties to the crime, and I think we need to talk with the good doctor."

"Do you think this has anything at all to do with the horse?" she asked.

"I don't know yet," Chang said. "But I always say that the only way to arrive at clear answers is to ask clear questions. Will you help me question Dr. Gianni? I know from the feds that he was cooperative with respect to your investigation of the dead stallion, so I think it might be best if we question him together."

"Fine, I'll call him," she said. "Now what's the deal with the suicide note?"

"Chet left one on his kitchen table. It's authentic according to his wife; although she's not saying much of anything without her lawyer. That's a question that I'm hoping your doctor friend can help us answer—where the hell Chester Pawlek is, and is he dead or alive?"

Chapter 30

Anthony Gianni pulled into the gate of Midway Farm in the pre-dawn hour. There was a crisp chill in the air, a typical autumn morning in Kentucky. Dr. Steven Highet had already spoken to the gate attendant so that Gianni would be cleared for entry.

The jet black Porsche Carrera 4 was covered with road dust from the long drive down the various interstate highways from New York to Kentucky. It pulled up in front of Barn 5, where Highet stood alongside his truck, loading some instruments into the rear cargo area. He regarded the sleek lines of the Porsche and smiled at Gianni. "You always were a car nut, even in college. How long did the trip down take?"

"Around eight hours I guess. I left around 6 p.m. last night. Stopped at a little motel outside of Charleston, West Virginia, just before midnight. I slept for a few hours and left there around 4 a.m."

"Eight hours from New York? Did you drive or fly?"

"A combination of the two, I guess. The roads are pretty empty in the late evening and early morning hours, so with the radar detector on, I do move right along. I don't get to drive this all that often. I still have an old Jeep for my daily driver."

"So where are we headed first?" Highet asked.

"Clay City," Gianni answered.

"You really want to go to that little hick town? You've got to be kidding."

"I am not. I want to try to locate that hermit, the one your student helper told you about. We can at least snoop around a little and see who might know something about him. If there is any chance of a link between him, the characters at the landfill, and Chiefly Endeavor, then I want to find him."

"Anthony, listen. It's little more than a hunch from a college kid. The police have totally discounted it."

"Which is precisely why we can't."

"All right. Why don't you let me drive though, we can take the truck. That hot rod of yours in Clay City will attract more attention than a priest in a whorehouse."

"I'll drive the 911. We'll be fine."

They simultaneously boarded and fastened their seat belts. The engine started with its characteristic guttural sound and Gianni drove slowly out of Midway Farm and onto Old Frankfort Pike. Once they were on Interstate 64, he picked the pace up to a steady 90 mph, only occasionally throttling back to 75 when the radar detector beeped.

"So you said you had actually heard of Clay City when we spoke last week," Highet said. "How in the name of God could you know Clay City?"

"Believe it or not, Janice is a Kentucky native and she actually grew up not too far from there, on a small farm near Winchester. Though to see her today, you'd sure as hell never guess it. Somewhere between Winchester, Kentucky, and Manhattan College, she started to morph into this Westchester wannabee. And today, well, let's just say she was a lot more likable in those leaner days. The girl I married was a lot closer to a "have not" than to the entitled bitch that I live with today."

Gianni glanced to his right and saw a sadness take over Highet's face. "I'm sorry, Steven," he said. "It's insensitive of me to sit here and complain about my wife like that. How long has it been now?"

"She died five years ago, and I still miss her terribly. We had our share of disagreements too, mostly over my ridiculous work schedule, but I miss her more than you can imagine. I still spend some of my nights sifting through old letters and other memorabilia."

"I'm sorry, Steven."

"Forget it, really."

There was hardly any traffic when they turned off I-64 and headed southeast on the Mountain Parkway, another divided highway, towards Clay City. It seemed deserted for a four lane, divided highway. Highet glanced over at the digital readout on the speedometer. "Is that ninety?" he asked.

"Yeah, about," Gianni said.

"I hardly feel it. This damn thing is rock solid," Highet said.

Gianni glanced in his rearview mirror, noting a plain-looking sedan not more than ten car lengths back. He slowed the Porsche down to 80, then to 75, and the sedan continued to maintain a constant distance between them. The radar detector was silent, so it was unlikely that it was an unmarked police car.

"Okay, Steven, hold on because you're about to feel it a little more now." He downshifted the manual gearbox from sixth gear into fourth, and quickly accelerated as he shifted back up through the gears to sixth. The digital speedometer now read 120. Trees on the side of the highway moved past the windows in a blur, and the Porsche passed three lone vehicles as though they were standing still.

"I think we're being followed," Gianni said.

Highet looked at Gianni, then at the speedometer. Gianni's hands gripped the wheel securely at the nine and three o'clock positions. Highet then turned to look through the wide rear window of the Porsche. At 120 mph, the sedan still appeared to be closing on them.

"He's coming up on us," Highet said. "What the hell kind of car is it that's able to keep up with us at this speed?"

"Probably some modified police cruiser. But it's no cop, that's for damn sure."

"How do you know?" Highet said.

"Because I would have been stopped long ago. It's not a cop."

Gianni saw the vehicle in his side mirror now, in the passing lane and closing in, even as the speedometer read 125. "Steven, there's a gun under your seat. Reach down and get it."

"What?"

"I said there is a gun under your seat. Reach under your seat and grab the gun, NOW."

Highet reached under and brought out a silver handgun, a Beretta 90-Two. Gianni applied the brake steadily but firmly and the sedan soared by, then slowed down to again position itself alongside the Porsche. The sedan then made a series of erratic but deliberate turns directly into Gianni's path, attempting to force him off the highway. Gianni met each of the assaults with a counter maneuver, swerving and managing to avoid the sedan and still maintain control of his car. It helped that he had slowed to about 80 mph during these continued assaults. Suddenly he downshifted and accelerated past the sedan. At 110 mph the vehicle was still on his tail and once again pulled alongside. The tinted window on the passenger side of the sedan opened and a gun barrel emerged.

"God damn it," Gianni yelled and once again put the gas pedal to the floor. He managed to pull about four car lengths ahead of the sedan. Then in a bold and sudden move, he forcefully hit the brakes. The sedan flew by and Gianni pulled the Porsche onto an exit ramp at a speed that Highet must have thought would end in a fiery crash. Instead, the Porsche accelerated and stayed glued to the road like a roller coaster on a ramped, sixty-degree turn and with the same kind of g-force felt deep in the gut of the two riders. Where the exit ramp straightened, Gianni hit the brakes hard and the Porsche screeched to a halt, careening across an intersection before finally coming to a complete stop at the opposite side of the cross road.

Highet flung his shoulders back into the seat, his head firmly against the high head restraint. Slowly he turned to look at his old college buddy.

"Holy shit," Gianni said.

"Thank God Almighty," Highet said. "I guess we took the right car after all."

Chapter 31

"Now what?" Highet asked.

"I'm going to pull into that station. I need some water or something."

"Do you still want to go to Clay City?" Highet said.

"We're almost there. I say we may as well move on. Our friends in the police cruiser are probably half way to West Virginia by now. I doubt if they'd bother heading back. There are too many different routes off this exit."

"Shouldn't we call the police?"

"I don't know yet," Gianni said. "Just let me collect myself." He got out of the car and went with Highet into the small convenience store attached to the gas station. Outside the door was a newspaper stand containing copies of the *Lexington Herald-Leader*. The headline instantly caught Gianni's eye. He walked inside and paid for two bottles of water. Outside, he fed two coins into the newspaper dispenser and removed a single copy. The headline read:

WITNESS TELLS ABOUT FINDING
SLAIN CLAY CITY POLICE OFFICER

MOUNT STERLING—Something wasn't right about the way Randy Lacy's police cruiser came down U.S. 15 toward Stanton on June 13th. The Clay City police chief's car went airborne for a few yards before it landed in a ditch off the side of the road.

Seconds after the car stopped, a handcuffed James H. "Jamie" Barnett kicked out the back window of the cruiser, crawled out and attempted to jog away, drivers who were the first witnesses at the scene testified Thursday. It was then they knew that something terrible had happened to Clay City's sole police officer.

The article and some related pieces went on to describe the bloody crime in which the officer was shot with his own gun following a DWI arrest. The defendant was thought to have links to a growing drug trafficking problem and a crystal meth lab operating in Powell County.

"It appears there is quite a lot of activity in this little town," Gianni said.

"I know," Highet said. "That murder was big news, even in Lexington. The police chief was a very well-liked fellow. He often was known to cuff suspects in front, because he thought it was more humane. He probably thought this guy was so intoxicated that he wouldn't be much of a threat. But the guy hid the police officer's gun while the officer was outside the cruiser, and then shot him with his own gun while he was driving down Main Street."

"Sure sounds like a nice place," Gianni said.

"You made up the itinerary, Anthony."

"I know, and we *are* going there today."

"You know," Highet said, "I've never liked guns, never wanted them around. But I think I've just changed my mind. This may just be the week I get myself a gun."

"Not a bad idea, and it's a hell of a lot easier in your state than in mine," Gianni said. He looked at the photo of the suspect in the paper. He was a man in his thirties with deep-set, dark eyes, pale and gaunt cheeks, wild, unkempt shoulder length hair and a scruffy goatee. He handed the paper to Highet. "On to Clay City," he said.

They approached a diner on Main Street in Clay City, an all brick building with a large, old-fashioned storefront window. It looked like it might have been one of those Rexall® storefronts in years past. Gianni parked the Porsche amidst an assortment of pickup trucks and rusty jalopies, down the street at some distance from the diner. He hoped no one in the diner would notice the vehicle. Both he and Highet were dressed in jeans, work boots and clean but casual cotton shirts, so he hoped they would blend fairly well with folks in the diner and that he might be able to speak with some of them.

They walked in the door and a dark haired, slightly plump lady greeted them cordially. "Morning," she said. "Sit yourselves anywhere ya like."

They took a seat near one of the large front windows and surveyed the tables in the diner, then looked out to the street. The patrons in the diner did not seem to pay much attention to them. It was apparent that most of them knew one another and appeared to regard the two newcomers as strangers but not necessarily intruders.

Gianni and Highet reached for two plastic-covered menus that were standing up between a glass sugar container and a napkin dispenser. The waitress came to the table with pad and pencil in hand. Her dark brown hair was piled high onto her head, in a sort of beehive that reminded Gianni of a favorite aunt, long since gone along with the hairstyle, or so he had thought. She chewed her gum energetically.

"Whatcha fellows want?"

Gianni had not really read the menu, but he ordered first in a rather automatic or unconscious manner. "Can I have an egg white omelet with mushrooms, home fries and dry wheat toast?"

The waitress stopped chewing her gum for a moment and cast a sideways glance at Gianni. "No egg whites, hon."

"Um, okay. Mushroom omelet then."

"Home fries or grits?"

"Home fries, please."

"Coffee?" she asked.

"Sure, thanks," he said.

Highet ordered a hotcakes breakfast special from the menu, orange juice and coffee. The waitress returned with the drinks and asked rather cheerfully, "So what brings you all to Clay City?"

Gianni answered, "Well, believe it or not, my wife grew up in Winchester."

"No kidding," she said. "So what brings you to Clay City then?"

"I'm trying to locate an old friend for her," Gianni said. "I think he's rather well known around here. They refer to him as the old hermit."

"Sure. I know him," she quickly replied.

Gianni could barely disguise his excitement. "Oh really?"

"Sure, he'll come in once in a while. Why are you looking for him?"

"Well, my wife…she knew him a long time ago, before he became such a loner."

"Where's your wife now?" she asked.

"She's…sick." He deliberately and somewhat instinctually crafted the lie. He thought it might evoke some sympathy, and he was right.

"I'm sorry. So is this guy like an old lost friend or something?"

"Sort of."

"Well I'll tell you what I do know," she began. "He lives around here in the woods somewhere. I can't tell you where, because I don't know where. But he didn't always live like that. He used to teach at the University. Science…Genetics, I think. He owned horses too, race horses. Then his wife got very ill. Some kind of lung problem, she had.

"What kind of lung problem," Gianni asked.

"Don't know. She never smoked, neither. He used to come in more often back in those days. He would talk a little about her needing a lung transplant, and about how he was saving up for it because insurance didn't want to pay for it. He was in a big fight with them too, but he had some money saved from his horse business and he was trying to set aside every penny he could for his wife's surgery. Only she died waiting for the operation, and he was never quite the same after that."

Gianni looked across the table at Highet. For the second time that morning, Highet's eyes were noticeably filled, and he was looking up towards the ceiling in an effort to contain the tears.

There was a long silence. Gianni looked away from Highet towards an empty wall with a vacuous expression on his face. Then he spoke directly to him, even though the waitress was still at the table. "That's so sad," he said. "And it's odd." He looked up at the waitress. "My wife had a sister-in-law who also died not too long ago, waiting for a lung transplant. She had pulmonary fibrosis, actually. She never smoked either."

Highet spoke next. "I never knew that, Anthony. It must have been very difficult for Janice to see her brother and his wife go through that."

"No, it wasn't really. Janice hasn't seen her older brother in over ten years."

Chapter 32

When Gianni drove back into the entrance to the Griffin Gate Hotel in the early afternoon, two police cruisers were parked near the hotel entrance. Outside the vehicles, a pair of Kentucky troopers paced along the walkway, talking to one another and to two men at the bell captain's stand. Gianni felt his heart race. His first thought was that someone he had passed at breakneck speed had called the police, and that they had somehow tracked his location. He avoided the front circle and parked at some distance from the entrance. He was alone, having left Highet back at Midway Farm.

As he walked towards the hotel entrance, the two troopers converged on him, blocking his entry to the front door.

"Dr. Anthony Gianni?" one of them said.

"Yes sir?"

"We're from the Kentucky State Police and we'd like to have a few words with you."

"About what, may I ask?"

The door to one of the police cars opened and Lt. Terri Jones approached the trio.

"We meet again, Doctor," she said.

One of the troopers said, "We want to speak with you about Chester Pawlek. We can make this informal. Would it be okay if we just go to your room to talk? Or else we could go back to our post in Frankfort."

"No, we can talk here."

The two officers introduced themselves as troopers Johnson and Boggs. They had the same grey and black uniforms as New York's troopers, Gianni thought.

They all walked in a group through the hotel corridors towards Gianni's room on the first floor. The walls throughout the hotel were liberally furnished with paintings and photographs, most with an equestrian theme. A few of the hotel guests turned to consider the four as they walked by in silence.

They stood awkwardly in a cluster at one end of Gianni's room as he gathered two chairs from the patio and two from the room, placing all four at a round table near the sliding glass doors. They sat down in the cramped quarters, as if preparing to play poker at a table that was far too small.

Boggs was the older of the two troopers. His hair was mostly grey, close-cropped and combed straight back from the forehead. He and Lt. Jones began the questioning.

"When is the last time you talked to Chester Pawlek?" Boggs asked.

"I can't recall exactly when it was." Gianni thought back to their meeting in his office, shortly after the Catroni boys had performed the mini amputation on his finger. He wondered how much he should tell them. Just answer the questions, he thought, no need to volunteer anything. Just handle it like he would if he were sitting in court as an expert medical witness.

"What was the nature of your last contact? Was it a business or a social visit?"

"We met in my office because he had some medical questions he wanted to ask. They were veterinary issues really, but he was looking for someone with some medical background to help him."

"Help him with what?" Detective Jones weighed in.

"He had some questions about the equine herpes virus."

"Interesting," Jones said. "Was that meeting before or after you and I spoke?"

"It was before."

"But you never told me about that meeting when we spoke before."

"You never asked," Gianni said.

Jones' eyes narrowed. "Do you know that Chet is missing, that he left a suicide note at his home?"

"What?"

"How long have you been in Kentucky, Doctor?"

"I drove down last night."

"You haven't seen any of the news about the missing New Jersey mobster and the dead man hanging in his house?"

"I've seen virtually no news for the last week or so. I catch a little radio in the morning, usually NPR or Imus. That's been about it. I told you the last time we met that I have been a little obsessed with the death of that stallion. Between that and my medical practice, I've barely had time to eat."

"Dr. Gianni, your office informed us that your departure this week was rather abrupt. I called them because I had originally planned to travel to New York and meet you there along with the detective in charge of investigating the Pawlek disappearance."

She brushed back a loose strand of hair that had fallen across one eye. "Your office informed me that you cancelled several patients because of an emergency out of town. What was the nature of that emergency?"

"I told you. I have been very wrapped up in the mysterious death of the stallion, Chiefly Endeavor. Dr. Highet and I have been in close contact, but I needed to see him face-to-face again."

"Do you always drive from New York to Kentucky in the middle of the night, Doctor?"

Look, I have nothing to hide and I am trying my best to be cooperative with you. But right now, I don't like this line of questioning. You said you wanted to know what I could tell you about Chester Pawlek. I obviously know a lot less than you do about his present status. Chet is someone I generally try to avoid."

Gianni looked at Jones and then at the troopers, doing his best to match their cold stares.

"So if you are now making this an interrogation about me, then I am going to insist that I have legal representation present."

"Did Chester seek your opinion on any other medical matters or facts," Jones asked.

"I don't know what you mean."

"Do you keep insulin in your office, Dr. Gianni?"

"No. And this interview is over."

Chapter 33

Delores Pawlek stood in her enormous kitchen and looked at her son John, slouched over the granite-slab breakfast bar. He looked awful. His once muscular frame was at least ten pounds lighter. His face was pale and gaunt. When he had first come in, she thought she noticed pinpoint pupils. Perhaps she was looking too hard, she thought.

He cast a perfunctory glance her way and said, "I hope he *is* dead."

"How dare you. He's your father, John."

"By blood, maybe."

"What has gotten into you?"

"What's gotten into me? How about the fact that I can't pretend to have any feelings for him just because there's a chance he may be dead. I can't forget all the bullshit, his arrests, the beatings and the lies about how they happened, all the times he left in the middle of the night and never came back for days. What's gotten into you?"

"We had our rough times, but your father was always a good provider."

"A provider of what? Of all this shit here." He gestured wildly with his arms. "All this useless crap."

"He's putting you through college right now, young man."

"Oh my God, I cannot deal with this. Just tell me what they told you."

"They found his car abandoned in Westchester, in a ditch near the train station in Ardsley. The train station is right on the river. There was a note in the car, almost like the old one. Except this one also said *Death by drowning is painless.* It's his writing and it's for real. He was obsessed with that theme from M*A*S*H: *Suicide is Painless.*"

"And suppose they don't find a body, then what?"

"I don't know. Your Uncle Ralph already stopped by with some cash. He said how sorry he was and that he had instructions to make sure we had everything we needed until things were straightened out. Instructions from your father, I mean."

"He's not my uncle, Ma. Stop calling him that. How much cash?"

"Enough for awhile."

"Just great. A friggin' Mafia annuity."

"Stop right now. I'll hear no more of that, John."

"So what will they do, dredge the whole damn river from the Tappan Zee to Jersey City?"

"I'm not sure. They're investigating. That Chinese detective wants to question us again." She took off her glasses and raised them to the light, squinting as she inspected them, then blowing away tiny specks of dust.

John said, "God, you sound just like him, now. Doesn't the Chinese detective have a name?"

"Chang," she answered. "I had a call from that doctor too, the Italian one he owned the horse with." She started to pick at her blouse with her thumb and index finger.

"What did he want?" John asked.

"I'm not exactly sure. It was a very strange call."

"I can stay here with you tonight, but I'm going to my room now."

"Don't you want some dinner? You need to eat." She stood up and walked over to the oven, a shiny, stainless steel Viking. "I made some nice lasagna in my new oven."

"Maybe later."

WHEN THE MUSIC became too loud and too metallic for her to stand any longer, she knocked on her son's door. There was no answer, so she let herself in. She thought she saw John sleeping, slumped over a beanbag chair. His eyes were partly open and he had a look of utter contentment on his face. She felt happy for him until she looked beside his outstretched arm and saw a rubber tourniquet and a small, tuberculin-type syringe, the kind her mother used for insulin injections. His eyes opened a little more, and then rolled back in his head.

"John, my God!"

His head lifted just slightly. He smiled at her and waved her away. "I'm fine...my music...fine."

The sight startled her at first, though she wasn't overly surprised. She simply regarded it as one more destructive tentacle that she could trace back to Chester Pawlek, bringing her one step closer to despising the man she had married.

Chapter 34

When Gianni drove up to the gatehouse at Midway Farm it was barely light. He knew he would find Highet on his morning rounds and he would see him one last time before heading back to New York. The gatehouse light was off and he didn't see the attendant.

He got out of his car, looked in the window and saw the attendant on the floor. A stool was overturned, and it was lying between his legs. The small Mexican man had a slash across his neck, extending from ear to ear, partially decapitating him. Blood had splattered everywhere within the small hut, as if the man had spun in circles—all the while spewing blood—until he finally collapsed on the floor.

Gianni reached for his cell phone to dial 911 and for an instant, he thought about getting back into his car and just driving. He surveyed the once white, painted surface of the hut's walls, painted now with blood that in some areas still hadn't dried. Gianni knew that the drying time of blood could vary, but was generally less than fifteen minutes. *He was just here. I just missed him.*

The Kentucky State Police were the first to arrive. Gianni felt relieved that neither of the two troopers who had questioned him the previous day was on duty for this call. Joe Travers, the farm manager, had also arrived. While one of the troopers secured the crime scene, the other began to question Gianni and Travers.

Gianni looked at the trooper's name plate: *Larson.* He was a young sergeant with a Nordic look, blond hair, blue eyes and a narrow face. He didn't introduce himself by name, only that he was from the Kentucky State Police.

"Who was first at the scene," he asked.

"I was," Gianni replied.

"What time?"

"Just about 6:00 a.m."

"And you?" he said, looking at Travers.

"Just now, same as you," Travers said.

"What's the man's name?"

"Alvaro," Travers answered. His first name was…he went by Gus. Gus Alvaro."

"How long has Alvaro worked here?" he asked.

"Several years. He was a good man, a good employee."

"I assume he has all his papers?"

"Probably an H-2B Visa, but I'd have to check."

"You better do that. Did he have any enemies that you know about?"

"No, I think he was pretty well liked."

"Any family?" The trooper asked.

"None that I know of, not here in the States anyway."

"Girlfriend?"

Travers paused. "There were some rumors about Gus."

"Rumors about what?"

"Some of the other workers said Gus was a homo."

"Homosexual?"

"Yeah," Travers said. "They talked about him and this guy at the dump, the guy they call Zoom. That guy would come around here once in a while. I never liked him. In fact, he was around here the morning our stallion died. You, I mean, the police brought him in for questioning then, didn't they?"

Larson ignored the question and continued. "What else can you tell me about Gus and Zoom? Were they homosexual lovers?"

"How the hell would I know," Travers snapped. "But if they were, then things were pretty tense lately."

"Why do you say that?" Larson asked.

"Well, this is just talk around the barn, you know. But Gus had told some of the workers that he knew something about the Zoom guy, something really bad. He said it was something he wasn't sure he could keep to himself. He was a good man, and I think he was feeling really guilty about it."

"You said Zoom sometimes came onto the farm property here at Midway?"

"I saw him here twice and threw him out both times. We have a lot of very valuable horses here and we try to run a tight ship," Travers said.

"So how did he get on the property?"

"Well, like I said, there were rumors about him and Gus."

"So did you talk to Gus after you threw Zoom off the property?"

"Yeah, gave him holy hell. And the last time he was real upset, like he wanted to confess something but he didn't. Then I started to hear more rumors that he knew something bad about Zoom, something that was just eating at him."

"But you have no idea what it was?" Larson asked.

"No idea, and now…we may never know," Travers said, looking back at the gatehouse.

As the trooper was walking back to his car, Gianni's cell phone rang. He glanced at the caller I.D. *Restricted.* He assumed it would be Janice calling from their home number, and for the first time in a long while, he actually wanted to hear her voice. He turned and walked a few steps away and flipped open the phone.

"Dr. Gianni?" a low, gruff voice said.

"Who is this?" Gianni asked.

"Go back to New York," the gravelly voice said.

"What?"

"I said, go back to New York. You're not needed around here. There is no business for you here in Kentucky. Stop nosing around and go back to New York while you still can."

"Who the hell…" The caller hung up and the call ended.

Chapter 35

While Gianni and Joe Travers were at the gatehouse with the state police, Ryan Fischer was starting his morning chores in Barn 32. An unmarked police cruiser pulled up alongside the barn and two men emerged from the vehicle. Both men were at least six feet tall. One had a muscular frame and short dark hair standing mostly on end. He had a long scar on the right side of his face, extending from alongside his eye, down towards the corner of his mouth, ending near his shirt collar. The other man had a huge frame, but he was burly and fat, not muscular like the man with the scar. His baggy chino pants were held up by wide orange suspenders, and he carried a four-pronged pitchfork in his chubby hands.

The pair walked slowly down the shedrow, looking into each stall. In one of the stalls, Ryan was using a pitchfork to remove manure from the wood shavings and straw remnants, pitching it into a wheelbarrow at the stall door. He hummed a tune as he worked.

The fat man stopped in front of the wheelbarrow. "Mucking

stalls?" he said.

"Yeah," Ryan answered, startled by the stranger. He hadn't noticed the pitchfork at first, but he noticed it now as the man leaned on it, his huge hands now beside his head, clutching the tool as he smiled at Ryan.

"Are you Ryan?" the fat man asked.

"How did you know that?"

The man grinned and bounced his head side to side, his fat face almost looking friendly. "I just know," he said.

Ryan could see the man with the scar standing at the stall door now. Unlike the fat man, he had a mean and penetrating gaze. There was no mercy in those eyes.

The fat man said, "You've been snooping around the dump, talking to those guys that live there."

"I just bring the garbage there. I talk to them a little."

"You know Mahlon?"

"I know who he is," Ryan answered.

"Mahlon told you about the hermit."

Ryan was silent.

"This is all shit you better just forget, kid."

The man with the scar grinned. His teeth looked like big white squares. "Do you know how you can just forget certain things?" he said.

Ryan shook his head in terror.

"Because we can help you forget," the fat one said, still smiling and shifting his grip on the pitchfork. I mean, I could take this pitchfork," he said, raising it and then moving it to one side, holding it like a spear. "I could take it and plunge it right through your fucking heart. But I really don't want to do that. I mean, you seem like a pretty good k-kid."

Ryan had recoiled to the far corner of the stall, and the fat man was inside the stall door now.

"I only give one warning, kid," the fat man said.

The two men then left quickly. When they reached the end of the shedrow, Ryan ran to the last stall and peered around the corner at the dark-colored vehicle as it skidded down the gravel lane, spitting gravel and raising a trail of dust.

HIGHET ARRIVED AT BARN 32 sometime later, accompanied by Gianni, who was still visibly agitated from the scene at the gatehouse. Ryan was sitting on the ground outside the entrance to the barn when Highet and Gianni walked up. Gianni was still recounting the horrific events of the past hour, but Highet raised his hand, cutting him off in mid sentence when he saw the boy.

"You look like you just saw a ghost," Highet said.

"Do I?" Ryan said.

"And it's not like you to be loafing on the job. Are you okay, Ryan?"

"Yeah, I'm…all right."

"Well I want you to meet a good friend of mine, Dr. Anthony Gianni."

"Pleased to meet you," Ryan said, getting up from the ground and extending his hand. Ryan's hand felt ice cold to Gianni and his face looked ashen.

"Ryan is interested in vet school, and I think he'd make a great doc," Highet said.

"He's one smart kid."

Gianni said, "Your detective work at the landfill was quite interesting to me. Can you tell me about the magazines?"

"Sure. There were two kinds." His voice trembled slightly as he spoke. "*Blood Horse Magazine* and the *Daily Racing Form*. All organized in neat piles with the newest ones on top."

"And someone told you they save them for the hermit?"

"Yeah. The guy they call Zoom told me that. His real name is…" He stopped abruptly in mid sentence.

After a long silence, Highet spoke. "Ryan, you may as well hear this from me. I'm sure the news will be all over the farm before long. The gate attendant, Gus, was found dead this morning. It looks like he was stabbed. Horrible thing."

Ryan's eyes began to fill and he seemed to be trying to suppress sobs. His neck and shoulders quivered.

Highet put his arm around Ryan as the sobbing continued.

"Maybe you should take the day off," Highet said. "I can tell Travers."

"No. Can I shadow you today, all day?"

"Sure. Just let me finish with Dr. Gianni. He needs to get on the road."

"I'm done," Gianni said. "I've told you all I know."

"Will you call me when you get back to New York?"

"I will, but then I'll be out of touch for a while. I made the commitment months ago to go on that medical mission. They line up a ton of surgeries for me to do. I can't renege on it now."

"Where are you going?"

"St. Lucia."

"Isn't that a resort island?"

"It's a resort if you happen to be one of the Americans or Europeans who can afford to stay in the four star hotels. Most of the natives are dirt poor though. There's a hospital on the southern part of the island that relies on volunteers for at least half of the medical care. Like a lot of Caribbean islands or resort areas, if you venture off the tourist track, you'll see abject poverty, and the natives are plagued by some very rare medical conditions. I'll see adult patients with cleft lips or palates, completely unrepaired. They live with conditions that would be unthinkable in the developed world."

"You should take a trip to rural Kentucky," Highet said.

"I'm not saying we don't have medical neglect right here, but it is different. In any case, this is the worst possible time for me to leave the country for two weeks, but there's no way around it."

"I think it's wonderful that you're doing it, Anthony. Plus, the change of scenery may do you good."

"It will be tough to stay in touch. But I'll check my email daily and I can always use the phone at the hospital if we need to speak."

"I'll let you know if there's anything major."

Gianni looked at Ryan again. He thought the boy just looked ill. "Steven, I'm off. You better take good care of our future vet now."

Chapter 36

Flying into St. Lucia, the Pitons twin volcanic peaks can be seen rising a half mile straight up from the water's edge. Gianni looked out the window, then back at the snoring face of the stranger to his left. He had wanted Janice to join him on the mission. She could have done volunteer work at the hospital or the local school. It would give them one last chance to reconcile, away from the trappings of success that distracted them both. Perhaps the girl from Kentucky would resurface if she were suddenly forced to help those in need and to witness the destitution in the small town of Vieux Fort.

Janice wouldn't hear of it. She had deals to do at home. Gianni had begun to wonder if they were all real estate deals.

He shed his blazer as he walked off the plane and felt the thick, humid air. It was oppressive, not very pleasing, even though he had left New York's cooler temperatures earlier that day with no regret.

He collected his baggage from a disorganized heap at one end of the Hewanorra Airport and quickly cleared customs. When the customs agents had heard he would be volunteering at the St. Jude Hospital, there were no more questions. As soon as he stepped outside, he was approached by a friendly-looking man with a round, brown face and a bald head. He spoke with an accent that Gianni assumed was native St. Lucian.

"Dr. Gianni," the man said.

Gianni turned toward the voice, startled to hear his name. The man had just picked him out of a crowd of tourists.

"I am Guy Montoute. So nice to finally meet you."

"How did you know me?"

"Oh, I could just tell," Montoute said.

Gianni remembered that he had been required to submit a photo as part of his application. Perhaps that was how he was recognized. Still, there was something strange but comforting, almost saintly about the man. He felt it the moment they shook hands.

He followed the man to a small SUV, a Suzuki, Gianni thought, as he headed to the right side of the vehicle.

"Do you expect to drive, son?"

"I forgot," Gianni said, noting the steering wheel on the right side.

"You like to be in control of things."

"Why do you say that?"

Montoute looked at Gianni and just smiled without answering. Another man acting in a similar way would surely irk Gianni. This one did not.

"This place will do you good," Montoute said. "We have much work for you, but you will relax too."

They headed out on a tortuous course over a rough dirt road.

The edges of the road were deeply rutted, and dogs and cats roamed free along the side of the road. In one open area, a solitary cow grazed on sparse patches of grass. There was no fence around the field, but the cow was secured to a tree by rope and collar.

Close to the road, there were tiny shacks of wood or cinder with furled tin roofs, crumpled at their edges. They passed a group of young children walking along the road with bare feet, laughing as they went.

Gianni thought of all he had left behind—his busy practice, Janice, and the escalating violence and intrigue surrounding Chiefly Endeavor. Perhaps when he returned, he would have a clearer picture of the things in his life he should keep and the things he should leave behind.

The dirt road ended at the entrance to the hospital. A gate blocked the entrance and a guard raised the gate when Montoute's vehicle approached.

"You will find the St. Lucian people to be quite friendly," Montoute said, seeming to once again read Gianni's thoughts. "But like anywhere, there is a certain element outside the gate. If you ever feel threatened, just say that you are working at St. Jude's. They will respect that."

The facade of the hospital had a raised bridge connecting the second floors of two separate buildings. A sign beneath the windows on the bridge read:

Come share with us the service of giving love, care and hope to others.

Built during World War II by the U.S. Army, the buildings were painted a dull yellow, with maroon extending from ground level to the bottom of the first story windows.

"Come, we will take your things to your room and I will show you around," Montoute offered.

The room featured a twin bed on a metal frame, and a small wooden desk with an unmatched chair. An electric fan sat on the desk, next to a single window with thin, pale blue curtains tied in the middle. A tiny closet had a half-dozen old, bent-up wire hangers on the rod.

"The bathroom and shower facilities are in the next building over," Montoute said, pointing. "Let's go to the dining hall. It is almost time for dinner. You will find our meals simple but tasty. We do a lot with what we have. Very little meat, but always some nice vegetables and a starch. On Sunday many of our volunteers go to the village for dinner. So tonight, the dinner will be more modest."

In a corridor on the way to the dining hall, they passed a statue of Jesus in one corner. Light through a Venetian blind backlit the statue, giving it an ethereal quality. The face of Jesus was dark brown, like Montoute's, something Gianni had never seen in other renderings of the Christ figure.

"As I said, dinner will be light on Sunday. We have bean soup and bread," Montoute said, looking at a menu posted outside the entrance to the dining hall. "The water in that large boiler is safe to drink. You must not drink from the tap. The smaller boiler has coffee, all day long."

Must taste great, Gianni thought.

"I should let you have some time to yourself now. Some of the doctors and the other volunteers will be coming through for dinner. All of the new arrivals come on Sunday, so you will have a chance to meet your colleagues. Tomorrow I will orient you to the clinic and the operating theatre."

Gianni was tired from his trip. On his way out, he stopped to fill a cup with coffee. It tasted watered down, but it didn't have the bitter, burnt taste of coffee that stood all day. He hadn't eaten in at least six hours and would return in short order to a feast of black bean soup with chunks of baguette-style bread. Far more memorable than the menu would be his dinner companion, a charming doctor from West Sussex, England.

Chapter 37

When the doorbell rang, Janice Gianni set her glass on the table, stood up, brushed back her newly bleached blonde hair with pink, manicured nails and then unbuttoned two more buttons on her silk blouse.

She walked to the door somewhat unsteadily. Looking out the side window, she saw Brad Hill standing at her door. She opened the door and kissed him on the lips. In her high heels, she stood nearly eye to eye with the dapper publishing baron, dressed in a starchy, pink, button-down shirt, stiffly creased jeans, and Gucci loafers, no socks.

"Dom Perignon for the lady," he said, showing her the bottle.

"Gracious, what are we celebrating, Anthony's departure or the big payment on the dead horse?"

"Both, although I don't have the money just yet, you know."

They walked back into the great room of the Giannis' contemporary style home.

There was a fire raging in the fireplace, a massive stone structure extending from floor to ceiling. The smell of burning wood was pungent but pleasing, and the dry oak crackled and popped.

"Nice fire," Brad said.

"I start it with a firelog then pile on the seasoned wood that Anthony splits. You should see him out there with his ax and his chopping block."

Brad's eyes were drawn to one corner of the room, and he walked over to inspect a large, wooden gun cabinet with a glass front. Inside were at least six rifles and several pistols. A few looked like antiques. Brad pulled on the door and noted that it was locked shut.

"I knew Anthony did some hunting, but I didn't know he was such a gun nut."

"Oh God, yes. I'm so glad he's off saving the poor and wretched natives of St. Lucia. Do you know he actually asked me to go with him? He's clueless. I'm rather surprised he went himself. He's been so damn worked up over that horse."

"Ever shoot one of these?" Brad said.

"What? Oh the guns," she said. "Actually I have. Anthony thought I should know how to handle one, living up here in the country and being alone so much. Open the champagne, Brad."

"Guess I better behave," Brad said. "I wouldn't want you to pull one of those pistols on me." He walked to another area of the room where an oriental bar was open, another gigantic piece of furniture with a lighted and mirrored back. He came back with two champagne flutes and the open bottle of Dom Perignon.

"So I don't get it, Janice said. "We still don't know if Chester Pawlek is dead or alive, but you seem pretty sure you'll get the insurance money for Chiefly Endeavor."

"It doesn't matter if Chet's dead or alive because I hold the lien. They just need to complete the investigation for insurance purposes. It's only a formality."

"Suppose they find out something?" Janice said.

"The horse died from the equine herpes virus, Janice. End of story, stop worrying." He sat on the leather sofa and placed the two glasses and the champagne bottle on the glass table in front. "Come join me," he said.

"I just don't understand how that ruthless gangster signed over four million to a preppy, Ivy League publisher. A cute one though, I must say." She leaned over and kissed his cheek then sat next to him on the leather sofa.

"Well first off, he owes me the money. Let's not forget that I loaned him money for a whole string of high priced horses he bought in the auctions. Once he got that first good one, he couldn't stop buying. It was like a disease. So with interest, he basically owes me close to four million, and he'll get substantially more than that from his share of the insurance proceeds."

Janice crossed her legs and swung them up onto the sofa. Brad's eyes followed their movement and continued to inspect their tanned shapeliness.

"I've learned a few things about Chester Pawlek," he continued. "First off, he's a bit of a coward, especially lately. The last time we talked, he was a bundle of nerves. I learned early on what he feared most—intelligence and legitimate power, the kind of power I have. He fears what he cannot understand."

"Why did you even get involved with him? Why lend him the

money for the thoroughbred business in the first place?"

"Let's just say he offered a rate of return that no hedge fund manager I know can match. It was just another investment and it was backed up by a letter of credit from his bank. His credit was pretty good in those days, though things have clearly deteriorated since then. And that's why Chiefly Endeavor had to go. The insurance money is *my* payback."

"Are you sure it's really going to be yours, free and clear?"

"Perfectly legal, my dear. Now what about your brother? What's the latest?"

"He'll never talk," she said.

"I don't know about him," Brad said. "I still question his motives. I can't believe he came through for us. What the hell was in it for him?"

"Stop trying to understand his motives. Do you think a man who lives in the woods in Clay City is playing with a full deck? You've heard his rant about the thoroughbred species and how commercial breeding has destroyed the soundness of the horse. The great genetics professor! Furthermore, you mustn't forget how Chester Pawlek screwed him on that horse deal a few years back. He wanted revenge, and he had no idea that Chet would actually benefit from the stallion's demise. My dear brother has turned into a total loon. Just be happy that it worked to our advantage."

"You're absolutely sure he had no idea that Chet was in cahoots with us?" Brad said.

"No way. He would never do anything that would benefit Chet. For all he knew, Chet had all the money he needed and only stood to make a lot more if he could keep Chiefly Endeavor as a stallion—the type of breeding that my brother was sure would further weaken the breed of the thoroughbred horse. Chiefly Endeavor was retired at three because of soundness issues. It was just the sort of thing that nut in the woods felt he had some God-given right to stop."

Brad sat back into the plush leather sofa and toasted with his champagne glass.

"Here's to the smartest damn hermit south of the Adirondacks." He leaned over and put his arm around Janice, drawing her closer and whispering in her ear. "When Anthony got me into this business, I never dreamed what the rewards would be."

"Which rewards?" she said.

He turned her face to his and kissed her. Janice took his hand, urging him off the couch and crawling onto an afghan she had placed in front of the raging fire.

Chapter 38

"I'm Alice Bond, mind if I join you?"

Gianni looked up at an attractive blonde who appeared to be in her mid-thirties and spoke with a distinct British accent. She wore a surgical scrub top, short khaki pants that ended mid-thigh, and sandals. Her blonde, shoulder length hair had a soft natural curl. He had been seated alone at the table and she had taken him by surprise.

"Please do," he said. "I'm Anthony Gianni. There's certainly room." He waved a hand over the empty table. The entire hospital dining room was mostly empty. A few people had begun to file in through the open doors. Some looked at the menu posted outside and walked away.

"Sunday nights," she said, taking a seat across the table from him. "Just about everyone goes out for dinner. Some go to one of the local spots in Vieux Fort. A few splurge and go north to the Hilton for a very expensive feast at a four star hotel. For a lot of the

American tourists visiting the island, the Hilton is all they ever see. It is a gorgeous venue though, right next to the Pitons. It even has its own heliport so the vacationers can bypass the arduous trip on dirt roads, not to mention all those unsightly shacks."

"But they're missing this," Gianni said, looking at his bowl of black bean soup and broken pieces of baguette.

"Just get in?" she asked.

"A couple hours ago. Just enough time for the quick tour with Montoute."

"Ah, little Buddha," she said. "That's my personal nickname for that adorable little man."

"He did have a certain spiritual quality about him, I must say."

"So where is home?" she asked.

"New York. I work in Manhattan and live in Westchester, north of the city. How about you?"

"West Sussex in England. Do you know where that is?"

"Small world. I did a fellowship in East Grinstead many years ago."

"That's my hospital. You were actually there?"

"I did a fellowship in trauma surgery at the end of my residency," he said.

"General surgery?"

"No, Plastics. But it was the oral and maxillofacial guys who ruled the roost there. Most of what I know about trauma surgery I learned from them. How about you?"

"How about me?" she said, with her British inflection and a bit of sarcasm.

He looked up from his bean soup and saw that she was smiling.

He liked the sparkle in her eyes and the hue, an intense shade of green that matched the green color of her scrub top. "Well…how long are you volunteering? On what service and anything else you might care to add?"

"I'll be here three weeks in all. I just completed my first. I'm an anesthesiologist."

"Trained in England?" he asked.

"At the Guy's Hospital," she said.

"So you're a Consultant at East Grinstead now?"

"Yes. I see you remember the lingo," she said. A consultant in the British medical system was analogous to an attending doctor in the U.S. system. A resident doctor in England was called a registrar. Gianni also knew that in a reverse form of snobbery only the British could contrive, when one ceased to be a registrar and became a full-fledged consultant, one actually relinquished the title of doctor and became Mr. or Ms. again.

"So I guess we don't call you Dr. Bond, then?"

"They do here. In your case, I suppose Alice will do."

He saw the same smile and the sparkle in her eyes. She hadn't started on the soup she had carried to the table. As she tasted it for the first time, she said, "A good glass of merlot would improve this dish greatly."

"I guess I missed that in the chow line," Gianni said.

"Some of us keep a little supply in the dorm," she said. "Plastic cups, broken down lawn chairs, the starry sky…it has its own charm, you know."

"Is Andy Carr still at Grinstead?" Gianni asked.

"He is. Good surgeon, Carr."

"Yeah. He taught me a lot."

"Are you married, Dr. Gianni?"

Gianni didn't answer.

"Tough question?" she said. "Generally yes or no will do."

"I am," he said.

"Pity," she said.

"There's a lot going on now, that's all."

"Pity," she said again.

A thin smile crossed his lips. He wasn't sure whether he should consider her a cold-hearted Brit, or appreciate her for not prying.

"I expect we'll be working together tomorrow," she said.

"How do you know? Have you seen the operating room schedule?" he asked. "Oh excuse me, I mean the operating *theatre* schedule," he corrected himself, remembering the British traditions.

"I haven't seen the schedule," she said, pronouncing it 'shed-yule' in her proper English. "But I know we're together because I'm the *only* anesthesiologist. Their one full-time attending quit about six months ago, so they rely entirely on volunteers, and there's one nurse anesthetist who is an employee of St. Jude. As you might expect, they burn out pretty quickly with those doctor to patient ratios."

"So I'll see you tomorrow," Gianni said. "Any advice for the new guy in the OR?"

"A surgeon is asking a gas passer for advice? Well this is a first. Sure, I can offer a bit of advice. Expect things to move very slowly. That is, until the shit finally hits the fan, which it surely will at one point or another. Expect that a lot of the equipment will not work, or won't be available. Most of all, be flexible and be patient. Not easy for you surgeons, I know. It will be a new experience."

Chapter 39

Steven Highet peered out the front window of his house at the pouring rain—rain so heavy that it looked more like thick fog. A street lamp behind a tall hemlock at the end of the driveway gave the tree just enough illumination for it to be visible. Through the downpour, it looked more spectral than real.

The lights of the Mercedes in the driveway had been turned off, but the two men lingered in the car, perhaps waiting for the torrent to let up. Highet was expecting the visit from his old veterinary colleague, Dr. Ted Frunkle, though he thought he was coming alone. The two men emerged from the vehicle with umbrellas and ran to the front door. Highet opened the door and the two men entered quickly, the umbrellas dripping on the foyer floor.

"Don't worry about that," Highet said. "Just leave them in the corner." He extended his hand to Frunkle. "To what do I owe this great privilege, Congressman?"

Frunkle had left veterinary practice many years ago to run for a seat in Congress.

A well-connected Kentuckian who was also a doctor of veterinary medicine, he had secured the seat with relative ease in a district sustained in large part by the horse industry. For a brief time years ago, he and Highet had been in the same private practice.

"We can't stay long, and I'm afraid this isn't a social visit," Frunkle said.

The big man standing beside him was not introduced. He left his dark raincoat buttoned tight, the collar pulled up close around his neck. Water ran down the coat onto the floor. He stared at Highet but did not speak.

Frunkle continued, "As a former colleague and a great lover of thoroughbreds, I am very disappointed in you, Steven."

"What are you talking about?" Highet said.

"I'm talking about the death of the stallion, Chiefly Endeavor."

"What about him?"

"Steven, we know you killed him."

"What!" Highet shouted.

"You heard me. You may be able to fool some of your colleagues with your phony obsession to solve the supposed mystery of the death from equine herpes virus, and you may be able to fool that surgeon friend of yours from New York, but you can't fool us. Who else had such ready access to the virus?"

"Get out of my house."

"Who else knew exactly where there might be an outbreak of the virus. It would be so simple for you to swab one infected horse and transport it to another. Still, you went one step further, right to the research lab at the University of Kentucky. You thought that lab tech would never talk, but she has. She's ready to go to the police and tell them that she gave you access to her lab, which just happened to have cultured EHV available."

"That's not true. The only thing I ever did at UK was to act as a clinical consultant on certain research projects. What motive could *I* possibly have?"

"Oh, I don't know. Fame and fortune, maybe. Your name is all over the papers and the trade journals with this bogus investigation of yours. Then you were able to save a couple of younger horses who contracted the virus. You were the big hero. Did you infect them too? But we don't really need a motive, because we have a confession from the lab tech indicating that you took live virus from her lab."

"That's a goddamn lie, and I still intend to find out the true cause of that stallion's death."

"Well, the lab tech is prepared to give a deposition under oath. I will follow up with a press conference, commending her for her courageous stance and calling for the revocation of your license in Kentucky. That would be enough to suspend your license, at least temporarily. There goes your investigation. I see a better alternative, though."

Highet looked incredulously at the two men standing in his foyer, water still dripping off their long raincoats.

"There is a better way," Frunkle continued. "You give your final report to the authorities and the insurance investigators now. No delays, you just end it. Conclude that the cause of death was the equine herpes virus and that there was no foul play."

"Get the hell out of here, now!"

"I was afraid you might say that, Steven. That's why I brought my friend with me tonight."

The big man reached into his overcoat. He pulled out a piece of paper and then spoke for the first time. "I got this address here, you see. It says 174 S-S-South Locust Road."

Highet felt his face flush. It was his daughter's address in Lexington.

"Mean anything to you, Doc.?" The man had a sickening, vicious looking smile on his fat face.

The two men turned to walk out the door. They stopped to retrieve their umbrellas and Frunkle looked back at Highet. "You see, Steven, it's just got to end now. It's best for everyone."

Chapter 40

Gianni reported to the Surgery Clinic at eight o'clock in the morning. It was a dimly lit room with four open bays containing treatment chairs with torn upholstery. Some but not all of the bays had old-fashioned medical floor lamps with gooseneck extensions; others had no auxiliary lighting.

Two nurses, native St. Lucians, greeted him cheerfully. They introduced themselves by first name, Suzana and Amara. Caribbean music was playing on a small plug-in radio.

"Your first patient is in the second bay," Amara said. "We are here to assist in any way we can. We are so happy you are here."

Gianni had read the background information about the hospital, the local customs and the limited resources. He knew they would be counting every last gauze pad, wasting nothing. He would be using many items that would be past their expiration dates, such as sutures and medications that had been donated from developed countries where such practices were forbidden.

Amara showed him around the clinic: the modest waiting area already full with patients, the sterilization area, and a tiny staff room with a coffee maker, small refrigerator and a metal table with three chairs.

"Every patient who comes here pays something," Amara said. We are proud people and we expect to pay as much as we can afford. I must tell you…do only what the patient asks, only what they came here for. You may see other problems that need treatment, but those things must wait for another time. The patients only expect to get what they have come for, what they have paid for."

Gianni thought, *I guess they don't provide free Viagra, like Medicaid does in New York State.*

In the second bay, there was a boy who looked to be about ten years old. He sat on the tattered treatment chair and his mother stood beside him. One side of his face was distorted by a huge swelling that extended from the area just under the left eye to an area under the jaw line. The boy's brown skin was shiny and reddened from the tension of the swelling. A portion of it looked like a water-filled balloon that was about to burst.

Gianni looked at the medical record, a single 5 x 8 index card with the patient's name, address and a record number. There was a section for medical history that was blank. He looked at the patient's name at the top of the card: *Lavon Gonin.*

"Is this the entire record?" Gianni asked.

"It is a new patient," Amara answered. "I'll show you our whole system later. It's rather simple but serves us well."

Gianni thought about how medical records back at home seemed to expand more every year, mostly driven by lawsuits and

defensive medicine. The simple record in front of him reminded him
of a chart from the 1950s that he had once encountered while doing
some research. It was the record of an admission for a tonsillectomy
procedure and it consisted of only five pages. The same record today
would fill a binder an inch or more in thickness.

"Any fever?" Gianni asked the nurse.

"39 degrees. I wrote that in the chart," Amara said.

That's 39 degrees Celsius…roughly 102 Fahrenheit, Gianni thought.
He spoke to the mother next. "How long has he been swollen?"

"Four days, maybe more," she said.

The boy sat quietly, though he clearly looked ill and was likely
having considerable pain.

"Is he eating and drinking?" Gianni asked.

"Not for the last day or so."

"Can I look in your mouth, Lavon?" he said to the boy.

The child began to whimper. His mother scolded him in French
patois and he instantly became silent. It seemed to be difficult for him
to open, but Gianni could see that the inside of his mouth was also
swollen, and that he had a permanent molar tooth that was decayed
and broken off at the gum line.

"Are there any oral surgeons here?" Gianni said to the nurses.
"This is a very bad infection and it seems to be coming from a
tooth."

"There is one in Castries," Amara said. She only comes here
once every two weeks."

"How far is Castries?"

"Thirty miles," she said. "That's a two hour drive on a good day.
With the construction and repairs on the dirt roads now, it could be

twice that."

"Well, I suppose I can drain the abscess, but he's going to need general anesthesia and he'll eventually need that tooth taken out."

"Dr. Gianni, would you mind if I give you a little more local information? They can take care of the tooth later. We have only one staff dentist, assisted by whatever volunteer dentists we can recruit for a week or two at a time. As for anesthesia, there are many patients waiting, always patients waiting. I have seen them do cases like this one right here in the clinic. If you take him to the operating theatre, then all the others move down the list and everyone waits longer still."

"An abscess this big? On such a young boy? No general anesthesia?

"Some local anesthetic maybe," she said. "It looks like it's about to burst, no?"

"I suppose so," he said, studying the tense skin just below the boy's jaw line.

"Mother and I will help keep him still," Amara said.

Amara went to the sterilization area and came back with a crude surgical setup. There was a tray containing a syringe with a single carpule of local anesthetic, a scalpel handle with a blade attached, and a curved hemostat that could be inserted into the incision, then spread open to facilitate more drainage of pus. There was a single, three inch gauze pad and a small piece of rubber tubing, one inch wide, which could be placed into the wound to keep it open for drainage.

For an instant, looking at the stark surgical tray, he flashed back to that dreadful day when the man named Hector had cut off his fingertip. The simple setup looked strangely similar. He glanced down at the finger, fully healed, though still squarish at the tip.

Gianni studied the sparse assemblage of instruments and planned his approach. He could inject only the skin with the anesthetic. Injecting directly into the abscess would be far too painful, and the acidic byproducts of the infection would render the anesthetic useless. If he were quick enough, he could make a stab incision, quickly insert and spread the hemostat, then replace it with the rubber drain, all in a matter of seconds. He would have to be right on target.

"Can I have some betadyne or alcohol," he asked as he donned sterile gloves.

Suzana, the second nurse, brought a gauze pad saturated with an orange-colored antiseptic solution and placed it on one side of the tray.

Gianni gently wiped the solution on the boy's swollen face, barely touching it. He placed a sterile cloth drape below the swollen area, covering the neck and shoulder area. The boy began to whimper ever so slightly. Again the mother scolded him in French. Gianni reached for the syringe and carefully injected a small area just underneath the skin. He had to work quickly now. The child began to cry loudly as Gianni reached for the blade. Then without warning, the mother grabbed the boy's arm and bit it, clutching it like a dog unwilling to release its favorite toy.

Gianni pierced the tense red skin and pus exploded out onto the sterile drape. Some landed on the lens of his safety glasses. He inserted the hemostat and seconds later replaced it with the rubber drain. With gentle pressure applied to the boy's face, pus continued to pour out. The boy continued to yell but did not move.

The mother released her clench on the boy's arm. A small

amount of blood was evident alongside the prominent bite marks. Once she released his arm, the boy let out a final, loud wail and fell exhausted into her arms.

Gianni, at first appalled by the mother's discipline, now realized that she had actually been a quick-witted assistant in the primitive procedure he had just discharged. He placed a sterile gauze pad over the drain and secured it with adhesive tape.

Gianni said, "He'll need to be on an antibiotic and I should check him again tomorrow. Can he remain in the hospital overnight?"

"If you order it," Suzana said. "Right now you are needed in the operating theatre. They just called down."

Chapter 41

By his fifth day at St. Jude, Gianni had seen an assemblage of rare and unusual cases. There were a host of benign tumors, marring faces with lumpy masses the size of grapefruits. While an untreated malignant tumor will too often kill its victim, benign tumors may grow to monstrous proportions, grossly distorting the face in the midst of their growth. He treated another patient with a huge upper jaw tumor that had displaced the orbital contents, pushing one eye upward and out of its socket, like some ghoulish rubber halloween mask. There were adult patients with unrepaired cleft lips, shunned or abandoned even in their native land. Then there was the boy whose nose had been partially avulsed when he was bitten by a rat. Gianni was especially pleased that the boy's first procedure had gone well.

Machete wounds were frequent on the island, as the machete was often carried to help clear passages through dense vegetation. On one of his first calls to the operating room, Gianni met a man in his early twenties with a huge facial laceration, an insult delivered by a machete-wielding compatriot early one morning, following a night-long drinking marathon. As he repaired the damage, he was once again reminded of his patient in New York City, the one that had never returned.

Alice Bond provided the anesthesia for these complex cases, with aplomb, particularly in view of the limited resources. She also continued to provide a source of distraction. At one point, when she noted him doing his best to contend with a stiff neck brought on by an operating table that would simply not adjust to his liking, she offered him a neck massage. It sounded like *mass hodge* when spoken in her proper English. Gianni declined, proceeding instead to the library to check his email.

The hospital had a rudimentary library with two computer stations that could be rented by the half-hour. Gianni paid for an hour and when he checked his Hotmail account, his attention was immediately drawn to an email from Steven Highet.

> SUBJECT: *Urgent update*
>
> *Anthony,*
>
> *There has been a new and frightening development. We need to talk. Call me as soon as you can.*
>
> *Steven*

GIANNI RAN NEXT DOOR to the Administration Office. There were two phones, and both were in use. He went back to his computer station and sent a reply to Highet's email

> *Steven,*
>
> *Phones here are impossible. I'm going to town to buy*

a cell that will work from the island tomorrow. Write
more detail in an email now!

He hit the send button and thought, *Be there now. Be at your*
damn computer.

Then like an anxious and slightly irrational child, he continued
to hit the refresh button every half minute, looking for a reply. Within
two minutes, he had one.

> *Anthony,*
> *Go to the AOL Instant Messenger site. Link below.*
> *If you haven't used it before, pick a screen name and*
> *we can text in real time (something my daughter*
> *showed me years ago). My screen name is Horsedoc.*

Gianni followed the link and within a minute, he was ALG2
looking for his old buddy horsedoc in cyberspace.

ALG2: Horsedoc?

Horsedoc: That's me. I just remembered your middle name…
Louis.

ALG2: Good memory. Now what the hell is up?

Horsedoc: I had a visit from our congressman in Lexington—
Ted Frunkle. He used to be a vet and we practiced together for a
while. He was with another guy…some fat thug. They basically told
me to close up my investigation of the Chiefly Endeavor death and
to conclude there was no foul play. Then the thug made reference to
my daughter Carla's address.

ALG2: Describe the fat guy.

Horsedoc: About 6 feet, 2 inches. Balding, with a big head and a round face. Big burly guy, but more fat than muscular. He had a bit of a baby face, at times almost friendly looking, but other times having this mean, penetrating stare.

ALG2: Damn it. What did his voice sound like?

Horsedoc: He barely spoke. But when he recited my daughter's address, he stuttered. I remember…it was so frightening. I was hung on every syllable. He stuttered when he was giving her address.

ALG2: It's Chet, Chester Pawlek. The bastard is alive.

Horsedoc: Anthony, what do we do now?

ALG2: You have to go to the police.

Horsedoc: But they threatened my daughter.

ALG2: You secure your daughter. Move her somewhere, not with you though. Then go to the police and insist on a 24 hour watch for her.

Horsedoc: He came with a goddamn congressman. How do I know the police won't be on the dole?

ALG2: Call Detective Jones. She'll involve the FBI. We can't fight this alone any longer. This guy is on the most wanted list. He's a ruthless killer. He'll kill again.

Horsedoc: What if I just do what they want?

ALG2: Don't do it. Don't think that you or your daughter will be safe just because you comply. They'll come back again to destroy their chain of evidence. I know how that bastard thinks.

Horsedoc: There's more. That last morning you were at Midway, two men terrorized Ryan, the boy you met at the barn. One of them was a fat guy who threatened to put a pitchfork through his heart if he didn't stop snooping around. It sounds like it was the same guy who came to my house.

Gianni was overtaken by an insurmountable sense of dread. He did not message back right away.

Horsedoc: Anthony…you there?

ALG2: I'm still here. Steven, go to the police and secure your daughter. Chet probably killed the gatekeeper that morning at Midway before he went on to Ryan.

Horsedoc: My God, why the gatekeeper? Why would he kill the poor gatekeeper?

ALG2: At this point that's for the police to determine. But I did overhear the farm manager tell the police about some supposed link between the gatekeeper and one of the guys at the dump. Come to think of it, you better keep Ryan away from that landfill from now on.

Horsedoc: The poor kid has been a wreck. He's with me or Travers all the time. He won't go anywhere alone.

ALG2: I wish to God I could be there. Promise you will call the police as soon as we're done here.

Horsedoc: I will. When do you come back?

ALG2: I still have another week. I'm totally conflicted and I want to finish up earlier, but I can't leave just yet. You won't believe the things I'm seeing here. Be careful, Steven. I'll get that cell phone tomorrow.

As he walked from the library back to his dorm room, Gianni paused again in front of the statue of Jesus. The lighting appeared different this time, coming more from the front of the statue. The venetian blinds behind the figure had been closed tight. Over the loudspeakers, he could hear the voice of Guy Montoute delivering the homily for the afternoon chapel service. The halls of the old military facility were full of loudspeakers, and Montoute's voice reverberated from one hall to the next.

Chapter 42

The old man left his bicycle on the side of the road and approached the entrance to the Clay City Diner. He carried a large, sealed manila envelope and a plain file folder filled with old magazine articles. He had a thick, white beard that had only recently been trimmed short. Two days earlier it had been a matted, unruly mess. His thin face was weathered and deeply crevassed, with blue eyes that still imparted a certain dignity despite his rumpled clothing, the faded corduroy pants and an ancient tweed sport coat. He had kept them for no particular reason and for the fleeting return to civilization today, his old professor's garb seemed to fit the occasion.

At ten-thirty in the morning, there were no other patrons in the diner. He had intentionally caught the down time between breakfast and lunch, knowing that Millie would be working.

"You clean up good, Wayne," she said, seemingly surprised by the new groomed look.

He stared at her with a somber expression on his face. "I have business in Lexington," he said, then he handed her the sealed manila envelope. "I expect to be arrested once I make my confession. You can read about it in the paper or watch it on TV. It will be headline news. But if you don't read of my arrest or if, failing that, I don't return here again on Friday, then I want you to deliver this to the Kentucky State Police."

She looked at the sealed envelope, then back up at the old man's face. "This is serious stuff," she said.

"Life and death," he said. "And five million dollars in insurance money."

She felt the thin manila envelope. "In here?"

"Not the money, just the explanation," he said.

"Whoa, wait a second now; we better sit down and talk."

"That's why I picked a quiet time," he said.

"Get you a coffee?" she asked.

He nodded and took a seat on a round, swivel stool at the counter. She brought him black coffee and pulled up her own bench seat, facing him from the opposite side of the counter. She touched her beehive hairdo then folded her hands on the counter and looked directly into his deep blue eyes.

He began, "In that envelope is the culmination of the last two years of my life, and my confession to a master crime. It has been a little more than two years since Sarah died. I committed the crime to avenge her death."

Her hands were on her chin now, and her eyes were still fixed on the old-looking man. "Crime?" she asked.

"Do you remember when I told you about her rare lung disease?"

"Of course," she said. "And you told me the bastards at the insurance company wouldn't pay for her surgery."

"Exactly. She needed a lung transplant. She had...it's called pulmonary fibrosis. That surgery was her only chance. So I saved every penny I could. I owned some race horses in the old days... before I chucked it all. One of them was doing quite well. I sold a major interest in that horse to this guy from New Jersey, some big construction guy. Only thing is, I never got the money like I was supposed to."

"Wait," she said. "There were two guys in here asking about you a while back. One of them said his wife was your long lost friend, trying to track you down and all."

"Anyone who tried to track me down in the last few months was surely not a friend. Someone tried to burn down my shack this week. They nearly destroyed it and the few possessions I still call mine. Last night I had to stay in the motel down by the Mountain Parkway." He looked down at the file folder stuffed with magazine articles, opened it and began to thumb through its contents.

"The story is all in here," he said, "but let me tell you why I helped them kill that big, powerful horse. I did it knowing that I would eventually confess and end up in jail. There's no one left in my life that I can tell, no one else that I can entrust with this envelope. I have no children, no relatives at all except for my sister Janice. There was only Sarah."

He pulled out a magazine article that featured a photograph of Chester Pawlek, profiling his success in the thoroughbred business. "This is the bastard who swindled me out of a modest fortune. I'm a geneticist, not a businessman. I understand horse pedigrees and I understand science. But I ended up losing every penny that I had saved for my Sarah's lung surgery."

"My God, I'm so sorry," she said.

"I signed over my ownership in a world class race horse and the bastard never paid me. So I tried to hire one of the best lawyers in Lexington to get my money back. Next thing I know, I'm threatened by some hired thug from New Jersey, and my lawyer suddenly gets cold feet and says he can't help me." He pounded his fist on the table several times, hitting the photograph of Chester Pawlek. "She died two months later. That's when I made my vow."

"Your vow?" she asked.

He pulled another article from his folder. "This is another horse called Chiefly Endeavor. It was the pride and joy of that bastard." He pointed back and again pounded the photograph of Chester Pawlek. And my dear sister and her husband were part owners in this one, until the horse was retired to stud."

He screamed as he spoke now, "Retired at the age of three!" He pulled out another article that was at least ten pages long. "The thoroughbred horse has been destroyed by the commercial breeders. A horse wins a few races, goes lame, they retire him and he goes on to produce more very fast but inherently unsound babies."

She appeared somewhat frightened by the rage in his voice as he continued to speak, more to himself than to the waitress now. "So Chester Pawlek had to pay, and what better way than to destroy his weakling stallion, Chiefly Endeavor. But I went one step further. I found a way to destroy his horse and to see to it that he would never see a penny of the insurance money."

He looked up at the ceiling. "My fickle sister Janice thought it was all about hatred for Chester Pawlek and my crazy obsession with the evils of commercial breeding, but it was so much more. It was really about avenging the death of my wife. No one will benefit from the stallion's death, because it was an act of fraud that killed the horse. I conspired in it, and now I must confess to complete the scheme."

"You'll go to jail," she said.

"So will Chester Pawlek, and my sister and her publisher friend. For them it will be hell. For me, jail won't be all that different from my solitary existence the last two years. I expect it will be a low security prison. I can read. I can think, and write. You know something, Millie, I don't even miss the money now that it's gone. Without health, and family, it means nothing. Most of all, I can take comfort that I have once and for all avenged her death."

He reached for another group of articles. "Equine herpes virus," he said. "It's a deadly disease in a susceptible animal. It's also highly contagious. A nasal swab from an infected horse is all it takes."

"So that's how you did it? A swab from one horse to another?"

"No, I did try to follow the outbreaks in Kentucky for some time, thinking that's how we would do it. But in the end, I devised an even more surefire method. I used some of my old contacts at the university to obtain live virus from the research lab. Of course, that did require a sizable cash payment, provided quite readily by my sister and her crooked publisher friend."

"So you all worked together then?"

"They thought we were working together, but I had my own agenda all along. They certainly never expected that I would turn around and confess, and turn them in at the same time."

"I didn't think you were talking to anyone lately, Wayne."

"Only when I had to. I do keep a PO box, you know, and I still have contacts. I have my ways."

"What about the fire?" she said "Someone must know what you're up to."

"I expect so," he said, "and that is precisely why you must promise me that if I don't get to the authorities, then at least this envelope will."

"So you were the one who actually swabbed the horse and killed him?"

"Not at all. I just arranged it."

"So then who actually did it?"

"It's all in the sealed envelope. Better you don't know who else is involved until I get to the office of the U.S. Marshall in Lexington."

"How are you getting there?" she asked.

He pointed to the bicycle outside the window.

"All the way to Lexington?" she said.

"No bus service around here and I don't think I'll hop the freight train dressed like this. I've been riding my bike to Lexington a couple times a month for the last two years. I go to the general store near Midway, and then I get all my reading material from the recycling center at the landfill." He thumbed the folder with nails that were still caked with dirt despite his recent sprucing.

"I'll drive you," she said. "I'd like to see you get there alive."

"If you drive me then we have to entrust the envelope to someone else. We could both get killed, you know. I'll just ride my bike."

"No. I'll leave the envelope at home with my sister. I can leave work as soon as the boss comes in at eleven. Put the bike in the back,

I want to drive you there."

"Okay," he said. He walked towards the door to retrieve his bike. He opened the front door, then turned his head, looking back at Millie. "You know, everyone has secrets, Millie."

"I reckon they do," she said. "I reckon so."

Chapter 43

Chester Pawlek climbed the open wooden staircase to Carla Highet's second floor apartment. Perspiring and breathing heavily, his 230 pound frame caused each stair to flex slightly under his leather work boots. His faded, baggy dungarees were held up by his signature red suspenders.

As he climbed the stairs, he didn't know that Highet had called the police and that minutes later, the state of Kentucky would be one solid roadblock. He didn't know that Highet and Gianni had already assumed that he had murdered the gatekeeper at Midway. Chet had become so thoughtless, he didn't even consider that Highet would have alerted his daughter, or told her to leave her apartment.

Had Chet known any of that, he might have left Carla Highet alone. All he knew was that he had to stop Steven Highet's investigation of Chiefly Endeavor. Chet would collect the insurance money, pay off Catroni, and keep some for himself. Maybe he'd even throw Brad Hill a few bucks, though he was far more concerned with getting Catroni off his back. The little preppy pussy would just have to wait a while, he supposed, because the lien Brad thought he held on the insurance policy was, in fact, totally bogus.

Chet wasn't even sure what he would do to Carla as he neared the top of the stairs. She was simply the next stop on his list. He would sometimes change his method of assault on a whim, like the time he met a foe in the bowels of Penn Station, where the hobos slept. He planned a single gunshot to the head. Then he noticed hoards of huge rats scurrying around the filthy caverns. So he shot the man in the leg, barely wounding him. Then he found some old rope, bound the man's hands and feet, and dragged him into a dark cavern. He left him for the rats to eat, describing for the man how they would slowly devour his flesh, bite by bite.

As he reached the top step and turned to walk down the open deck towards Carla's apartment, she emerged from her door carrying a backpack over one shoulder. She froze when she saw the huge man blocking her path at the top of the stairway.

"What's your h-h-hurry, sweetheart," Chet said.

"I need to get to work," she said. "I'm already late. They're expecting me."

Chet saw the terror in her eyes. He smiled with that wicked grin, an expression that could be at once terrifying and disarming. He pulled his gun. "Let's go back inside, honey. Turn around and g-go back inside. I don't want to hurt you."

She opened the door to her apartment. Chet forced her inside, grabbed the door handle and closed it behind them.

"Have a seat over there," he said, pointing to a recliner chair. He was enjoying the terror in her eyes now. He watched her sit rigidly on the edge of the well-worn recliner. As he approached the chair, he thought he smelled perfume. He bent over and smelled her freshly shampooed hair, her loose curls still wet from the shower.

"I don't want to hurt you," he said. "I think I want something else." He still held the revolver in one hand, and with his other meaty hand he began to touch her face.

She started to cry and pleaded, "Stop. Please, just stop."

He set the gun on a table alongside the recliner, then pushed the table behind him, out of their reach. "If you're good then I won't need that," he said, pointing to the gun. He stood in front of her, released the suspenders off his shoulders, and unbuckled his trousers. He grabbed her face with his huge hands. She instinctively tried to resist, but her petite physique was no match for his bull force.

He hadn't intended this, just as he hadn't intended to tie up the man alongside the tracks under Penn Station. He was just reacting. He just did it, and he was so wrapped up in the moment that he did something else he virtually never did. He stood in front of Carla with his back to the door.

The door opened but Chet didn't hear it. His head was tilted back, his eyes closed, a sickening smile on his face. He didn't hear the slow approach of footsteps either. The sound of a familiar voice distracted him. "God damn you," it said. By the time he heard the pop of the gunshot he had already felt the sudden piercing pain at the back of his head. He slumped forward onto the recliner where Carla still sat. Then everything turned to blackness.

Carla screamed and stood up, pushing him back with her folded arms. He tumbled backwards, falling over the table where his gun still sat, then onto the floor. His eyes and mouth were wide open. Blood trickled from one side of his mouth and onto his cheek.

A separate puddle of blood began to form around his head. His countenance was now a blank stare.

Chapter 44

Dr. Gianni left the island of St. Lucia four days early. He had worked longer days than most of the other volunteer surgeons, finishing a huge backlog of surgical cases. Dr. Bond had been a skilled partner as well as an intriguing diversion, and while he had managed to deflect her advances, she occupied a good portion of his musings on the plane ride home. He expected they might meet again.

Thoughts of Alice Bond could not diminish his growing anxiety surrounding Chiefly Endeavor, his friend Highet, and Chester Pawlek. After their last contact, he had tried to reach Highet again, first on a cell phone he had bought on the island, and later by instant messaging. The phone went dead minutes after he bought it, and Highet had apparently not been at his computer to receive the instant messages.

Gianni was anxiously awaiting his landing in Miami, en route to JFK International. He could use his own cell phone there, first to call Highet, then Janice. He turned on the phone and dialed as soon as the wheels touched down.

Damn, his voice mail. "Steven, it's Anthony. I just landed in Miami and I have an hour or so before I fly to JFK. Call me, for God's sake."

He retrieved and dialed Highet's home number…voice mail there, too. He keyed the number for the Equine Clinic next.

"Dr. Highet is off this weekend," the operator for the answering service told him. Can one of the on-call doctors help you?"

"Is there *any* way to get in touch with him before Monday?" Gianni said.

"Well, I can leave a message on his cell phone."

"No, I already have," he said.

He called his own home number. Janice sounded cold, and hung over, he thought.

"So how's the missionary?" she asked.

"Fine. It was a wonderful trip. What's new at home?"

"Well…" There was a long pause. "Chester Pawlek is dead."

"What!"

"He was murdered."

"How?"

"And there's more," she continued, ignoring his question. "I may be in a bit of a bind myself. It seems my dear brother Wayne crawled out of his hole in Kentucky and made up this fantastic story about a conspiracy to kill Chiefly Endeavor. Brad Hill thinks that I may be under investigation by the FBI."

Gianni felt his temples pulse. "Brad Hill? What the hell is this all about, Janice?"

"It's nothing, Anthony."

"It's nothing? Look, Janice, I have to get to my next flight. Just stay put until I get home. Don't talk to anyone, understand. Now what happened to Chester?"

"No one knows, but it's all over the news. He was shot by someone in Lexington. That's all they're saying, the police are investigating."

THE THREE HOUR FLIGHT from Miami to JFK felt like the longest Gianni had ever endured. Normally he would read, or do some sort of paperwork and time would pass quickly. Not this time. He fidgeted and moved his legs in circles to keep the blood circulating. He flexed and relaxed his calf and thigh muscles. Mostly, he thought about what he would do once he landed in New York.

He decided he would drive to the backstretch at Belmont Park even before he went home. There were very few people he could trust right now. He wasn't even sure if he could trust his own wife. His friend Highet might be missing, or at least he wasn't answering his mobile phone, which was unusual for him. Chester Pawlek had been murdered in Lexington, which was presumably where Highet should be. There was no way of knowing if Carla Highet was safe.

So he would seek out Jeff Willard first. Jeff would surely know as much as Janice, perhaps more about Chet and any others in the racing community who might have made news in the last week. Above all, he could trust Jeff, and they could talk amidst the refuge of their horses.

Once during the flight, he lapsed into a restless sleep and had a recurrence of a recent dream, the one where Sal Catroni was dressed like a doctor, wearing the white coat and the surgical headlight, and carrying a chain saw. When Catroni turned on the saw and approached Gianni in the dream, he woke himself with a gasp, looked out the window of the plane and saw the Manhattan skyline beginning to take form off in the distance.

When the plane landed in New York, Gianni again switched on his cell phone and tried Highet. There was no answer and he had no new voice mail messages of his own. He dialed Jeff Willard.

"Jeff, I'm home and I need to see you right away. I can get to Belmont in a half hour. Can you meet me at your barn?"

"Well, I guess so, but it's almost four in the afternoon. Why the barn at this hour?" Jeff asked.

"I'm just back from my mission and I really want to check on my horses. Plus we need to talk, and that's as good a place as any. Most of all, I think I just need to smell some hay and manure."

"Okay, Doc. I'll meet you there. A lot has happened since you left. I guess it's best that we meet face-to-face."

He ended the call just as he reached the baggage claim area for his flight. The area along the baggage carousel was crowded with passengers, some pushing to secure a spot. Behind the row of passengers who crowded the carousel, a man with a baseball cap and sunglasses strolled casually back and forth from one carousel to the next, always turning to see that Gianni remained in his sight.

Chapter 45

Gianni retrieved his Jeep from long-term parking, headed east on the Belt Parkway, then north on the Cross Island Parkway to Belmont Park. He parked the Jeep alongside Jeff Willard's barn, next to another Wrangler, even older and more beat-up than his own. He knew it belonged to Harold, one of the peace officers for the New York Racing Association. He recognized the vehicle by its pale blue color and by the U.S. Marines sticker on the rear bumper.

"Afternoon, Doc."

"Hello, Harold. Why so late?"

"Oh, just a little skirmish in one of the dormitories, nothing major."

Harold Kalish was about 60 years old, a friendly fellow who did not appear outwardly tough. His hair was thinned and mostly white. Gianni had always made it his habit to chat with him on his early morning visits. Harold often spoke of his service in Vietnam and his expertise in the martial arts.

"How about you?" Harold said. "Not your usual hour either, is it?"

"I'm meeting Jeff Willard. Just got back from my missionary trip in the Caribbean. Have you seen Willard around?"

"I haven't, but I saw his new assistant trainer a few minutes ago," Harold said, boosting himself into the old blue Wrangler.

"New assistant?" Gianni asked.

"Alison McKensie. Jeff promoted her."

As the Jeep drove off, Gianni walked down the shedrow, looking into each stall. Near the middle of the shedrow, Alison sat in the office, a stall modified to function as a work station. It had a metal desk and chair and a tall metal file cabinet. A small television sat on a shelf in one corner, tuned to the cable racing channel. Alison was watching the finish of a race at Churchill Downs.

"Congratulations," Gianni said. "I heard about your promotion."

"Thanks," she said. "You know, I think I owe my promotion to Chiefly Endeavor. That horse really got me noticed because he was so damn hard to handle. But the two of us just clicked. That horse could get away from Jeff's strongest male rider, but not me."

"I remember. So, who looks good now?" Gianni said, looking at the barn roster posted outside the office.

"Well, we're training a nice two-year-old by Friends Lake. Just won an allowance here and we may try him in a stakes race at Churchill after Thanksgiving. Then there's Padre. He's still with us. He was second in the Bernard Baruch Handicap up in Saratoga, and we're trying to place him as a stallion. He reminds me a little of the Chief, only about ten times meaner. He's six now and ornery as can be. Very territorial. There are certain horses he just does not like."

"I remember that about the Chief. He had to be the alpha in the barn, right?" Gianni said.

"I swear to God, Doc, if Chief was here now, we'd have to keep them in totally separate barns. This Padre would kill another horse. I mean it. He put one of our grooms out of work for two weeks. It wasn't his regular groom, and he turned his back on the horse when he shouldn't have. Next thing you know, he's on the ground bleeding."

"The horse kicked him?" Gianni said.

"No, he bit him. He grabbed him with his mouth and lifted him right off the ground before he let go. I saw the whole thing... scary. He's even nipped me once or twice, but nothing like what he did to that groom. So I just remember what Billy Turner, Seattle Slew's trainer used to say."

"What was that?" Gianni asked.

"The story has it that Billy Turner used to let Seattle Slew bite him once a day, as long as he kept winning races."

Alison turned off the television and grabbed a folder from the desk, placing it into a satchel along with several copies of *Blood Horse* magazine.

"Which stall is Padre in?" Gianni asked.

"He's in number five, the one with the cone in front of it. We keep him close to the office, but away from the horses that seem to bother him. He seems to tolerate the grey gelding next door. Alison walked down the shedrow towards her car. She walked to the outside of the yellow construction cone that sat in front of Padre's stall, giving wide berth to the stall door. When she walked by, the horse reared and kicked the side of his stall, then looked out at Alison as she walked by. "You behave, you hear me," she said, pointing a finger at the horse.

After Alison left, Gianni walked in the opposite direction, looking into the stalls as he walked. He paused to look at a dark brown colt. *Looks just like the Chief as a two-year-old,* he thought. As he studied the horse's conformation, he heard footsteps behind him, crunching in the gravel trench alongside the shedrow. He turned to his right, expecting to see Jeff. Instead he saw a tall stocky man in a black leather bomber jacket, baseball cap and sunglasses. He had a pistol pointed directly at Gianni and he whistled a nondescript tune as he approached. As he drew closer, Gianni noticed the long scar on the right side of his face.

"Stay right there, Doc," he said. "Put your hands up."

"Who the hell are you?" Gianni said, slowly raising his hands.

"Friend of Chester Pawlek," he said. "Came to finish some of his business. Pity he couldn't do it himself, because he really wanted to." He removed his sunglasses and placed them into his coat pocket with his left hand. Then he began to remove his jacket, switching the gun from one hand to the other. He draped the coat over a railing that ran parallel to the shedrow, continuing to point the gun directly at Gianni's head. He stood less than ten yards away.

Gianni studied the scar on the man's face. "You bastard," he said. "You were my patient…Hector Giardini. I fixed your face after someone took a swipe with a machete. I remember your name. We tried to contact you because you never came back."

"Yeah, I got the letters," he said. "How touching."

"You prick," Gianni said. "Don't you know that Chester Pawlek is dead?"

"Of course I know," he said. "But dead or alive, my instructions are the same—Dr. Anthony Gianni has to die, because he knows too much."

"So shoot me, Gianni said. Don't expect me to plead for my life. Because the truth is, I don't feel that I have a lot to lose right now. I won't leave any orphaned children. Just one slightly fucked up wife. And a pretty good bank account that will mostly go to charity. If that's my legacy, then so be it."

"You've got pretty big balls, I must say," Giardini said. "Even when I threatened to cut your fucking fingers off a while back, you stayed pretty cool."

Gianni flashed back to that horrific day when the two men had kidnapped him from his office. In a sudden recollection he remembered one of the men saying, *I'm Sal Catroni, of the Catroni family, and this here is Hector. Hector was a medic in the marines. He's here to help you with some medical treatment.* He remembered the man's face covered by a ski mask, and he recalled the sound of his voice.

Gianni began to walk backwards, slowly, unconsciously retreating from the gun.

"Where you going?" Hector said. "You can't go anywhere. It's just you and me. And the horses." He matched Gianni's retreat with slow steps forward.

"Who's your favorite horsey?" Hector said. "You have one here you like as much as the Chief? Because I could kill that one too." He made a sudden turn and pointed the gun into one of the stalls. "Is this your favorite horsey? How about if I shoot this one right between the eyes and send him to the meat market. You like horse meat, Doc? I hear they go crazy for it in Japan."

Gianni stopped in front of stall number four. Directly behind him was the cone in front of Padre's stall. He continued his slow retreat backwards, walking just outside the cone, between it and the outer railing.

Hector walked faster, closing the gap between them. He walked inside the cone and pointed the gun into stall number five. "Is this your favorite horse? I think he needs to learn how to behave."

The horse reared and kicked the side of the stall. Hector pointed the gun into the stall, then back at Gianni. The horse's head came out of the stall and in one sudden movement his mammoth jaws opened then closed on Hector's chest and upper arm. The horse shook his head and reared, hurling Hector to the ground. The gun fell to the ground, and Gianni lunged forward and grabbed it.

The swashbuckling Hector Giardini was now face down on the ground, dazed, his white starched shirt turning red with blood.

"My turn now," Gianni said. "Stay down or I blow *your* brains out." He dialed 911 on his cell phone.

Chapter 46

John Pawlek's attorney leaned over and spoke quietly, close to John's ear. They were the only two in the conference room on the first floor of the Fayette Circuit Court in Lexington. Eric Carlin was widely regarded as the best criminal attorney in the state—Delores Pawlek saw to it that her son got the very best. Carlin knew when to speak quietly and when to be the courtroom orator. His longish grey hair was neatly combed back from a part just off center, and he was dressed in an impeccably tailored grey suit.

"Do you understand the charge against you?" Carlin asked.

"I understand. Second degree murder," John said.

"Okay, let's do this once more before we go in front of the judge. I need to know exactly what happened that morning when you followed your father to Carla Highet's apartment."

John looked weary. His attorney had arranged for him to at least appear clean shaven and well dressed for the arraignment, but a little grooming could not reverse the past few days of mental and physical anguish he had experienced while confined to a jail cell.

Carlin said, "I want you to start back in New Jersey. Tell me why you came to Kentucky in the first place."

John began, "The FBI suspected that my father was involved with the killing of the stallion, and they wanted me to wear a wire and then get him to talk about it. The first time I tried was at home in New Jersey, but my father had disappeared the very same day I was set up to tape him. He had supposedly committed suicide, though very few people believed that."

Carlin said, "I'm going to ask you to talk about the hanging and how you came to discover the body in the attic. I want to show how traumatic that must have been for you."

"Fine, I can talk about that," John said. "I was really strung out for a while after that, totally messed up. My Uncle Ralphie—this friend of my father's, not my actual uncle—he was really worried about me. My mother had gone to him for help. Ralphie eventually told us that my father hadn't committed suicide after all, that he was still alive and in Kentucky. He thought it would help to straighten me out if he told me."

"Did it?" Carlin asked.

"I guess so. I went back to the FBI and told them what I knew. They started their own surveillance and when they located him, they told me where he was."

"Did they tell you what they expected you to do?" Carlin asked.

"They still wanted him on a wire, talking about how he had killed the stallion."

"Why didn't they just arrest him at that point?" Carlin said.

"Supposedly, they said they didn't have enough evidence to tie him to the hanging at the house. As far as the phony suicide, there was no insurance fraud or anything. The only life insurance my father ever had was a bag of cash that Uncle Ralphie would show up with once in a while. They wanted him on the big crime, the insurance scam on the horse, and they saw me as their best hope with that."

"So they sent you to Lexington?"

"I went to Lexington where he was hiding out on this estate that belonged to the Senator...Senator Frunkle. I couldn't get near that place, so the best I could do was to tail him when I got the chance. He didn't leave the Senator's place very often. This one morning, I got a call from Agent Hollis. They had finally managed to set up surveillance, so they knew when he had left the estate that morning. They wanted me to confront him, to re-establish our relationship and then get him to talk. So I followed him, keeping as much distance between us as possible. His first stop was at a gas station, but I couldn't bring myself to get out of the car. Instead, I just kept following him."

"To the apartment of Carla Highet," Carlin said.

"Yeah, though I didn't know that at the time, of course."

"You waited until your father went inside the apartment?"

"I saw him pull his gun on the girl outside the apartment, at the top of the stairway. When they went inside, I ran up the stairs towards the apartment."

"Where did you get *your* gun?" Carlin asked.

"From Uncle Ralphie. We used to target practice and shoot tin cans in the woods behind our house. A few times, he took me to the shooting range, and last summer he just let me keep one of his pistols."

"Go on," Carlin said.

"I stopped by the door, then quietly opened it. I knew my father had pulled his gun on the girl and I was really scared. The first thing I saw when I walked through the door was his big, hulking frame standing with his back to me at the far end of the room. Then I heard that poor girl—those sobs, like she was crying—except the sobs were all muffled. That fat bastard had his pants dropped down around his ankles. I saw the gun on the table beside him, and I saw the girl now, seated in the chair in front of him. I couldn't think of anything but stopping him at that point. He had to be stopped. I crept up behind him, and once I was sure I had a direct shot at the back of his head, I fired. Right before I shot him I think I said, 'God damn you to hell.'"

"What happened next?" Carlin said.

"He tumbled forward, falling onto the chair where the girl… where Carla sat. She screamed, and all of a sudden she stood up and pushed him back. He teetered for a bit then fell backwards onto the floor. I stood over him, pointing the gun at his chest. He quivered once or twice, and then he was still. He was dead."

"What was Carla doing at that point?"

"She was sobbing, shaking. I put my gun down on the chair and walked towards her. She just sat with her hands over her face and kept sobbing and shaking. Then I called the number I had for Agent Hollis. When I didn't get any answer, I called the Kentucky State Police."

"I hope to have you out on bail today, John. You have no criminal history and the FBI will testify as to your cooperation with them. Fortunately, you have no drug arrests. I guess maybe Uncle Ralphie got to you in the nick of time. I believe this is a case of justifiable homicide, and I think I can convince a jury of that. We'll need to detail the long history of abuse that you were subjected to. We need to show how you acted in the defense of a helpless girl who was being held under extraordinary and very sinister conditions by a known killer."

"She was being raped at gunpoint," John said. "He would have killed her once he was done with her."

"I understand. For today, we may still need to agree to a relatively substantial figure for your bail, which your mother is prepared to post. So you should certainly be able to go home. I have a sense that the district attorney will ultimately agree with a lesser charge than second degree murder, and a reduced bail figure as well."

"Thanks, Mr. Carlin. I just want to get home. I need to go home."

Chapter 47

Gianni arrived home at about six o'clock that evening. He entered through the garage and walked down a corridor to the entry foyer. Janice's Mercedes was gone and the front door had been locked. He dropped his bags in the foyer, walked to the large oriental bar in the living room and poured a generous ration of straight whiskey. In the safety of his own home, he felt at ease for the first time since leaving the island of St. Lucia.

He still hadn't heard from Highet and that concerned him. But Chester Pawlek was dead, and the accomplice supposedly assigned to kill Gianni was in police custody. He sipped from the glass and listened to the Beethoven sonata he had started in the CD player. There was still no sign of Janice. He had asked her not to go anywhere. He would call her cell phone, but he needed another few minutes to sift through some details. For a fleeting moment, his thoughts drifted to Alice Bond.

The music played softly in the background, and he heard the

front door being unlocked. Janice would sometimes use the front door in lieu of the garage entryway. She liked their grand foyer with its polished marble floor. She would fling the door open and flood the foyer with the bright lighting from twin chandeliers that hung from the cathedral ceiling.

"Janice?" Gianni called. There was no answer. He looked towards the foyer and saw Brad Hill standing in the darkened hallway.

"Well, well, look who's back," Hill said.

"What are you doing here?" Gianni said.

"Oh, I come here often, Anthony. Don't you know that? I even have my own key now."

Gianni turned in his chair and saw that Hill had a gun pointed at him.

"Of course, you probably don't know that because you're so damn clueless," Hill said. "I bet you don't know I've been fucking your wife for the last two years either, do you?"

Gianni stood up and turned towards Hill.

"Careful there, doctor. I'm not ready to shoot you just yet, but if you force me to, I will."

"Why, Brad? Why are you doing this?"

"Why indeed. Because you know too much. Now that Chet is dead, you may be the only thing standing between me and my freedom. Do you know who Wayne Logston is?"

"That's Janice's estranged brother. She hasn't seen him in years."

"Well, Wayne decided that he was going to blow the whistle on our little plot. But there's not enough evidence to actually incriminate me, only Janice. It seems the absent-minded professor left a few details out of his report."

"What do you mean, your little plot?"

"Chiefly Endeavor. We killed your beloved animal. It was the only way I could see to get the money Chester owed me. He owed everyone money, including me. Several million actually."

Gianni felt the blood rushing to his face. For a moment, he thought of lunging at the gun, then in a controlled, deliberate voice said, "So who killed the horse?"

"I guess we all did, in a way. Chet, Janice and I all knew about it. But it was her brother Wayne who actually master-minded the thing. He was the one who obtained the virus from the university lab."

Hill shook his head and tightened his lips. "Then he decides to go to the authorities and tell it all. He is one crazy bastard. He's in police custody right now in Kentucky."

"So what good will killing me do?" Gianni said.

"Janice suddenly wanted to confess and tell you everything. So if you didn't already know too much, I fear you would before too long. I've already lost the insurance money—Wayne made sure of that. If there's fraud then there's no payment. But I can't go to jail. I'm used to a much more comfortable lifestyle, you see."

"And you expect Janice to take the fall for you? She'll go to jail and let you run free?"

"Of course I'm sure. She adores me. She'll do anything for me." Hill's face was beaming, as though he really believed what he was saying.

"So she knows you're planning to kill me?" Gianni said.

"Oh, no. I don't think she'd go quite that far. Like I said, she was going to spill her guts out to you, and while I can trust *her* to protect me, I don't believe I can say the same of you."

Gianni raised his voice, "You won't get away with this, you bastard."

"Sure I will. The mob is already after you, Anthony. So this will just look like the next in a string of mob slayings related to that damn stallion."

"Tell me one more thing," Gianni said. "Tell me who actually killed Chiefly Endeavor?"

"I told you that we all had a hand in it. But if you mean, who in fact physically swabbed the virus into the horse's nose?"

"Who did it?"

"It was some degenerate that lives at the dump, the landfill in Midway. They called him Zoom."

"How could some hillbilly that lived at the dump get past security and into the stallion area at Midway?"

"They apparently paid Zoom enough money—I doubt it took much. Zoom and the guard at Midway were lovers, you see. I expect the guard would have let him go right to the owner's mansion if he had wanted to."

Hill paused and smiled, that same smug expression of self-love once again evident. "Any crime involves some combination of a few basic motives, right? Money, love…or just plain sex, and revenge."

"That poor guard ended up slaughtered," Gianni said.

"Yes, he did. I didn't have anything to do with that one, though."

Gianni looked down at the ground, his face expressionless.

Hill pointed the gun and said, "Time is getting short, my friend."

"Drop it, Brad." It was a woman's voice speaking now, coming from the foyer behind him.

Hill turned his head slightly, still pointing the gun at Gianni. Behind him was Janice Gianni, clutching a pistol with two hands, her hands shaking slightly.

"I'm afraid I can't drop it," Hill said.

"It's gone too far, Brad. Drop it."

Gianni surveyed the two. Hill continued to point the gun at Gianni's head while taking furtive glances over his shoulder at the gun Janice was pointing at him.

"There is no way I'm dropping this, Janice," Hill said.

Janice took two steps forward then fired two shots at point blank range. One bullet hole opened at the nape of his neck, another through the back of his head. Hill fell to the ground instantly.

Gianni bent over and felt for a carotid pulse. There was none. He then looked back towards Janice. She was down on her knees and she had the barrel of the gun inside her mouth.

"No!" he screamed. There was a third shot and Gianni saw the flesh around her mouth and nose suddenly torn open. Blood poured from her mouth and there were fragments of teeth scattered about the shredded flesh. Her eyes remained open as she fell over to one side.

With tears in his eyes, Gianni instinctively positioned her to open the airway. He could see her chest rise and fall, her breathing still spontaneous. She had a palpable carotid pulse, though she had lapsed into unconsciousness. He dialed 911 from his cell phone and ordered an ambulance to 25 Hollow Ridge Road in Armonk.

Gianni looked down at her bloody visage. She needed to be

intubated soon, before the swelling could compromise her airway, and she needed to be supported with intravenous fluids. But like others he had seen who put a gun to their mouth, she would survive. She destroyed a large part of her upper face but missed the brain and would avoid the lethal injury she had presumably wanted. Had the gun been angled slightly differently, she would not be alive.

He could hear the siren of the approaching ambulance. Gianni thought of the team he would call in to operate and of the sequence of operations Janice would require. Were the victim not his wife, he would most likely be part of the team himself.

Two paramedics ran through the front door pushing a stretcher. One of them carried a bright orange emergency kit. Janice was barely conscious and her breathing had become somewhat more erratic.

"I'm a physician," Gianni said. "The man is dead. The woman—my wife—needs to be intubated. Self-inflicted gunshot wound."

One of the paramedics sat on the floor directly at Janice's head and straddled her with one leg on each side. The second medic handed him a laryngoscope, which he skillfully inserted from his seated position on the floor. In seconds, an endotracheal tube was in place, the cuff inflated and the tube secured with an anchoring device. An Ambu bag was used to deliver several rescue breaths, then she continued breathing on her own.

Another siren blared, and lights from a police cruiser streaked through the living room window. As the paramedics moved Janice from the floor onto the stretcher, two troopers entered the living room. Gianni started to follow the stretcher to the ambulance when one of the troopers intervened.

"I'm sorry, Doctor," the trooper said. "One of us can transport you to the hospital shortly, but we'll need to take your statement first."

Chapter 48

Montauk, NY – Six months later

As Gianni headed east on Old Montauk Highway at the eastern tip of Long Island, the road in the distance seemed to disappear straight over the dunes and into the ocean. The deep blue hue of the water contrasted with the lush greens of the dune pines, the beach grasses, and the yellow and white wildflowers. Gianni slowed the Porsche and looked over at Highet. He had just collected him from the train station in Amagansett. The two had not seen each other in over eight months. Gianni thought back to his first trip out east and expected that his friend was perhaps just as moved by the vista off to his right.

"They call it The End," Gianni said. "It's the end of Long Island, the easternmost point in the state. A bird flying due east from here would end up somewhere in Spain, I expect. How in the world did your daughter end up here?"

"She came here years ago with a friend from college and fell in love with the place. From what I've seen so far, I can understand why."

"She's here for the whole summer?" Gianni asked.

"Unless she gets tired of the horses and the routine at Rita's Stable. She needed a break from Manhattan. Said she'll do some writing, and I expect she can get a job with another literary agent when she's ready."

"How is she doing, Steven?"

"Fine, really. We spent a good deal of time together right after the shooting. We went to a quiet place just over the border in West Virginia."

"That was when I was frantically calling you on my way back from St. Lucia."

Highet said, "Sorry, no cell service where we were. I really just needed to get her away, to someplace quiet. She suffered a terrible ordeal that day in Lexington, but she's a strong, smart girl. She went for a little counseling and stopped after just a few sessions. Said she didn't need it any longer and I expect she knows what she needs and what she doesn't."

The narrow road dipped and curved, and Gianni continued the slow pace, allowing Highet to enjoy the passing seascapes. "You'll love the town," Gianni said. "None of the glitz of the Hamptons. It's still unspoiled, really."

Highet looked back and forth, on both sides of the road at the magnificent homes overlooking the ocean. "How's Janice?" he asked.

"As well as can be expected," Gianni said. "Four surgeries, two separate admissions for alcohol rehab, and now another recent relapse that we're not quite sure how to handle. Random drug and alcohol tests are part of her parole agreement. If she doesn't stay clean, she could still be looking at some jail time."

"You expect to stay with her?" Highet asked.

"I still don't know. It's so ironic, really. Here I am, the plastic and reconstructive surgeon. A good portion of my patients are women about the same age as Janice. Some are stunningly beautiful, but they see some minor flaw that they want corrected. Janice had just about gotten to that point right before the shooting. She worried about wrinkles and talked incessantly about looking old."

Gianni was silent for a moment, then continued. "Someone once said that our fragile bubble of comfort and privilege can be broken in an instant. Hers certainly was. She's so horribly deformed now that even the best surgeons in the country can only do so much. After four reconstructive procedures, the best we can hope for is that she will look something less than frightening, so that maybe little children won't stare. So that adults will stop sneaking glances when they think we can't see them."

"Then you actually plan to stay together?"

"I said I don't know. Funny thing, she's become a much nicer person since she lost her physical beauty. She would actually like to do something with her life, and I expect she will if she can stay sober."

"You must have at least thought about divorce," Highet asked.

"Steven, I've thought about divorce for the last four years. I'm still thinking about it now. But I won't divorce her because she's deformed. I'll divorce her because I'm not sure I ever really loved her. But regardless, I'll support her in every way possible. She deserves that."

"Does she?" Highet said. "She had an affair with a supposed best friend. She engaged in a plot to kill Chiefly Endeavor. And she's an alcoholic."

"Yes, and she also saved my life," Gianni said. "She shot the man who was about to kill me. Should I ignore that?"

"No, I suppose not," Highet said. "And I never quite understood—why wasn't she already in police custody on that night?"

"Basically, the authorities in Lexington were all so focused on the Pawlek murder that they took their sweet time acting on the details of the hermit's confession. And I'm sure they initially wrote him off as a total nut."

"Did you ever talk about the reason why Janice plotted to kill Chiefly Endeavor?" Highet asked.

"I never did. There's incredible irony there too. I spent the better part of a year totally obsessed with that horse, looking for the elusive killer, and one of them shared my bed every night. That still haunts me."

"There's another thing I never understood. When Brad came to your house that night, he knew all about the hermit and the confession, but none of that was news yet. How did he know what the hermit had told the authorities?"

"The hermit wasn't taking any chances. He had led Millie, the waitress in Clay City, to believe that she was the only one who had a copy of that fateful envelope, the one that detailed his confession. But he had actually sent another one to his sister exactly two days earlier. Janice naturally shared all the details with Brad, and that set him in motion. Meanwhile, Janice was having her change of heart, and trying to figure out a way to break all of it to me."

"Has Janice seen her brother?" Highet asked.

"She went down to visit him around the time of the sentencing. That man endured a lot. Chet Pawlek swindled him out of his life savings and his one chance at saving his wife. After she died waiting for the lung operation, he became totally consumed by revenge. His vengeance had such far-reaching consequences and in the end, accomplished nothing. I suppose I should detest the man, but I don't."

"That trial was big news in Lexington," Highet said. "He found himself before a pretty sympathetic judge. Two years felony criminal mischief, another two for hard insurance fraud, and I doubt he'll even serve it all."

Gianni said, "I'm sure it didn't hurt that some of his testimony helped bring down the two Catroni brothers. Any news on the young Pawlek kid?"

"They're still arguing on the venue for the trial. Personally, I don't think it matters where they try him. He has one of the best defense lawyers in the state, and he should find himself before a sympathetic jury no matter where it is. There won't be many tears shed over the death of Chester Pawlek."

"And I saw that Frunkle finally had to resign," Gianni said.

"Oh yes, our illustrious senator from Kentucky—Teflon Ted. Well this one finally stuck, and there should be enough to put him away for a long time."

They drove through the town of Montauk. There were no chain stores, no buildings more than two stories tall, no stop lights. Gianni stopped at a crosswalk near the main intersection. A young couple held a toddler between them, one hand each. The child looked back across the street at a candy store, trying without success to pull in the opposite direction. They drove through town, then headed north towards the harbor and the Montauk Yacht Club, where they would stay for the weekend.

"Rita's Stable is right there," Gianni said as they made the left turn. "Carla is planning on dinner with us, right? I know a fantastic place in the harbor area, Dave's Grill."

"Sounds good," Highet said. "Tonight I can leave the dinner arrangements to you and tomorrow, Carla is our guide. She has three special horses picked out for us and a trail that leads down to the beach."

"I'm glad we could make this little retreat together," Gianni said.

Chapter 49

It rained in torrents for most of that night, cutting deep ruts into the dirt road leading to Rita's Stable. The rain had stopped and the mid-morning sky was now a cloudless blue. Outside the barn, Carla was busy saddling three horses: one chestnut, another dark brown, and one roan with hints of blue.

"Morning," Carla said. "Great dinner last night. Thanks again, Dr. Gianni. Now, are you guys ready?"

"Of course," Highet said.

"The roan filly is a little high strung," Carla said. "That's Peggy, she's mine."

"How about the other two?" Gianni said.

"The bigger brown gelding is Dagwood, and the chestnut with the lighter mane is Blondie. You guys can take your pick. Dagwood and Peggy are both purebred quarter horses, and Blondie is part thoroughbred."

Highet looked at Gianni and said, "You pick."

"I'll ride Blondie," Gianni said.

Carla positioned a mounting block next to Blondie. Gianni used it to boost himself into the saddle, and Carla gave her father a leg up onto Dagwood; then she put her left foot in the stirrup of her own saddle and was still swinging herself over the barrel of the horse when Peggy started to trot off. Carla slowed Peggy and led the way to a trail that weaved through some shadbushes and pine trees, then crossed Montauk Highway and headed towards the beach.

When they reached the beach, Gianni and Highet moved up and rode astride the roan filly. As they rode further east, the gentle dunes rose higher, gradually changing to high cliffs of rock and sand. Rising above them were mansions overlooking the ocean. Some were close enough to be visible from the beach below.

"Who was it that said there's nothing better for the inside of a man than the outside of a horse?" Highet asked.

"Ronald Reagan," Gianni said.

Highet was silent for awhile then said, "If money were no object, what would you do each and every day?"

"I thought about that a lot when I was in St. Lucia," Gianni said. "I'd probably spend more time volunteering, doing missionary work. Overall, I'd treat more of the patients who most need my services, the real disfiguring maladies, cleft patients and the like. I'd spend less time with the ones who just want bigger breasts, higher cheekbones, or fewer wrinkles."

"How about the horses?" Highet asked. "Do you still plan to have some thoroughbreds?"

"Thought a lot about that too," Gianni said. "For now, I plan to adopt one or two retired thoroughbreds. The kind who tried their hearts out and just never quite made it at the track. I'll board them on a farm near my home, give them a good home. I have my first one lined up already. Stu Duncker called me about this beautiful chestnut filly. She's very well-bred but they've dropped her through the claiming ranks, and now she has sore suspensories and still hasn't placed in a race. Stu told me 'She's no good as a race horse.' To which I replied, 'That's okay, she'll be good for me'"

"They're no different than people," Highet said. "The haves and the have-nots. Are you ever sorry you got into racing?"

"Not at all. Obviously I'd like to be able to turn back the clock and rewrite the chapter on Chiefly Endeavor. But regrets for my involvement? No. I've met some wonderful people, Stu Duncker for one, and many others. I'll get back in at some point. Once you experience that adrenalin rush of your horse closing in on the finish line…it's a bit addictive, isn't it?"

Carla raised herself up in the stirrups and began a slow canter up the beach, leaving Highet and Gianni behind.

"You know what I do regret, Steven?" He raised his head, pointing towards Carla. "I regret that I never had the chance to see a child blossom into a beautiful young adult. She's a gem."

Highet looked up at the high cliffs and the mansions. "What makes you think you can't still have a son or a daughter?"

"I'm almost fifty. Janice never wanted kids, and that was probably a blessing in disguise. I'm not sure she could ever be the motherly type."

"Even now?" Highet said.

"Maybe now she could, but of course, it couldn't be her own any more. And she'd have to stay off the booze. That's still uncertain."

Gianni was looking up at the cliffs now. Carla had slowed Peggy to a walk again and was just about fifty feet ahead. "Paul Simon has a place up there somewhere," Gianni said. "And Dick Cavett."

"Don Imus too, right?" Highet said.

"Hell no. He loves to make fun of the Hamptons crowd, but I still say it's different here, way out east. You still listen to him?" Gianni said.

"He's on in the truck when I do my rounds every morning. Do you?"

"Since the 70s," Gianni said.

"Then you know how old he was when he had his son. He beat an addiction to alcohol and cocaine, remarried, had a son, and founded the Imus Ranch for kids with cancer, and he was a hell of a lot older than you when he did all of that. We can all have second acts, you know."

"Maybe so," Gianni said. "Maybe so. Now it's your turn. If money were no object, what would your next act be?"

"Well, I suppose now is as good a time as any to tell you," Highet said.

Carla could hear them now, and she turned and grinned.

"Tell me what?" Gianni said.

"I'm moving to New York and joining the veterinarians on the NYRA circuit."

"I never thought I'd see the day. I thought you were a converted southerner."

"I love Kentucky," Highet said. "But I also love my daughter. She's up here now, and…" He looked at Gianni, then at Carla, who grinned again.

"And what?" Gianni said.

"And I love Alison McKensie. She's here most of the year too."

Gianni looked stunned.

"Anthony, it's that kind of love that makes you feel like anything is possible. Do you know what I mean?"

"No...I mean...that's great, Steven. She's a wonderful lady. Not to mention, one of the best horse trainers around."

"I'm just about ready to purchase a yearling of my own and let her work her magic," Highet said.

Carla jumped off her horse and walked her filly to an area where the surf splashed over some jagged reefs, creating a foamy little cove replete with shells and shiny rocks. She moved the foamy waters with one of her boots, reached down, selected two shiny rocks and a pink colored shell, then placed them into her saddlebag. She looked out at the ocean, and then turned east towards the lighthouse, its beacon barely visible through the dense green foliage and yellow wildflowers. After a while, she turned back towards her father and Dr. Gianni and said, "Let's go home now, Dad."

Epilogue

Eastern Kentucky Correctional Complex
West Liberty, KY

Mahlon Oakes sat alone in his cell. He had just come back from dinner, if you could call it dinner. Some kind of casserole, carrots, green beans. The milk was never cold and the bread was always stale.

One of the other inmates had been a little rough on him today, but he didn't mind all that much. Most of the men called him Zoom, a nickname he encouraged now. He had actually come to like it. It made him seem tougher, meaner. When they called him Mahlon they were usually mocking him. Zoom didn't like to be ridiculed.

Mahlon Oakes knew how to get even though. Just like he did with Gus Alvaro, the gate house attendant at Midway Farm. How careless the police were to assume that Chet had killed Gus. They questioned Zoom of course, just as they had questioned him the morning after the stallion died. It's so goddamn easy to lie when people think you're stupid, he thought.

Then, after they questioned Ryan Fischer, they just closed the case. They figured it had to be that Pawlek and his gangster friend killed Gus before they went on to terrorize the boy at the barn. *The boy...I miss the boy. Found out he's going to vet school in the fall.* The boy was one of the few things he missed in prison. He had plans for the boy, but they never quite came to be. Perhaps he should have waited to kill Gus, and devoted more time to the boy, trying to gain his trust. But Gus really did have to die, and after that day, Ryan never came around again.

If it hadn't been for Gus, and for that goddamn hermit, he might still be on the outside now. The hermit would have to die someday too, he thought. *He'll probably be out of prison much sooner than me though. They stuck him in the low security joint. They say I may be in here for as long as five years. Not bad for murder though. And there's nobody that knows I killed Gus. No one still living, that is. So easy to lie when you're so damn stupid. Still, I'll get the hermit one day. Catch him by surprise and slit his goddamn throat, same as I did Gus. Watch the blood drain out of his goddamn neck. I wonder what he'll say right before I cut him open. It won't be the same as with Gus. Gus just cried. He said he loved me. How could I kill him, he said. The crying just made me madder. Made it easier to cut him.*

Mahlon thought about how the two doctors might have a little something coming too. *Yeah, the surgeon and the vet.* He thought they should have minded their own goddamn business. *I could go after another one of their horses. They sure love their horses. It was good to kill the big horse. We'll see. I'll be more careful next time.*

Won't leave anyone behind who can throw me in. I guess I shouldn't feel so bad, really. I did get away with murder.

Still, I miss the boy. I never got to know him like I wanted to. I won't hurt the boy though. When I return to Midway.

Colofon:

This book was designed using the Adobe Caslon typeface, originally designed by William Caslon (1720-1766). He based his typeface on Dutch models. This Adobe variant was designed by Carol Twombly.

Breinigsville, PA USA
25 August 2010
244224BV00001B/36/P